FOCUS ON THE FAMILY®

Christian Heritage Series

THE SALEM YEARS

P9-BZI-115

The Rescue

Nancy Rue

BETHANY HOUSE PUBLISHERS
MINNEAPOLIS, MINNESOTA 55438

A Focus on the Family book published by
Bethany House Publishers
A Ministry of Bethany Fellowship International
11300 Hampshire Avenue South
Minneapolis, Minnesota 55438

Printed in the United States of America by
Bethany Press International, Minneapolis, Minnesota 55438

Library of Congress Cataloging-in-Publication Data

Rue, Nancy N.
    The rescue / Nancy Rue.
       p. cm. — (Christian Heritage series ; 1)
    Summary: Josiah and Hope, two young Puritans living in Salem Village in 1689, befriend a Quaker woman and a Wampnoag Indian who are not accepted members of the community.
    ISBN 1-56179-346-9
    [1. Puritans—Fiction. 2. Christian life—Fiction.
3. Massachusetts—History—Colonial period, 1600–1775—Fiction.]
I. Title. II. Series: Rue, Nancy N.   Christian heritage series ; 1.
PZ7.R88515Re   1995
[Fic]—dc20   94-41917
                                           CIP
                                           AC

---

98 99 00 01 02 03 04 05 / 15 14 13 12 11 10 9 8

For my daughter Marijean,
whose love for history led me to Josiah and Hope

Chapter One

id you hear something?"

"No."

"Aye—*I* did!"

"It was a twig snapping—don't be a ninny."

"Aye, a twig snapping, like someone is following us!"

"Do you think it's your little brother? Do you think it's Josiah?"

The Josiah in question flattened his 10-year-old self in the mud at the base of the stand of bare trees that lined the Ipswich River and stopped breathing while three pairs of girls' eyes peered in his direction.

"I don't think so," Josiah's 12-year-old sister Hope said. "He isn't clever enough to follow us this far without our knowing."

Josiah raised his curly blond head in protest.

"There!" Sarah Proctor cried.

"What?"

"*Someone* is in those trees."

"It couldn't be Josiah," Hope said. "He knows if I ever caught him spying on me—no, if I ever told Papa he was out here running the fields instead of tending to his chores—he'd be skinned."

"Isn't that what *you're* doing?" Rachel Porter said. "Running the fields instead of tending to your chores?"

She giggled her high-pitched giggle, and Josiah heard Hope's husky chuckle join in. Under the cover of their laughter, he shifted in the underbrush. The spring mud along the river bank was seeping into his left ear, and several thorns had worked their way through his breeches and into his thigh. Rachel and Hope chattered on, but Sarah hushed them with her always nervous voice.

"I heard something again!"

"I tell you, it isn't my brother. He's a brainless boy."

"But what if it's something else? Or someone else?"

Rachel stopped laughing. "You mean, like a bear—or Indians? The Indians are savages. They'll torture you—my father said."

"Don't be a ninny," Hope said again. But Josiah heard the scared pinch in her voice, and he smiled against the mud. It was time for a move. Whatever sound he made, he knew Hope would hear it. She had the sharpest hearing in Salem, Village or Town. Slowly he stretched out the fingers of his free hand, grasped a fragile branch at the bottom of a birch, and snapped it.

There was a chorus of squeals.

"Run—!"

"Go—!"

"This way—!"

In a flurry of long skirts and shrill, frightened voices, the three girls tore off.

Josiah covered his laughter with his hand and forced himself to stay down until he was sure they wouldn't look back again.

All that noise would've drawn any bear or Indian right into their path, Josiah thought with a knowing smirk. And they said *he* wasn't smart.

That thought pulled him out of the mud. *He isn't clever enough to follow us this far without our knowing,* Hope had said. He could prove her wrong—and he'd have plenty to tell William Proctor and Ezekiel Porter when he saw them.

Josiah squinted into the early afternoon sun and watched the girls' white caps grow smaller amid the trees across the river upstream. Usually William and Ezekiel planned the following of the sisters that the three boys did together. But he was alone today—with no one to tell him to hush and do as someone else said. Now was his chance.

Every free minute last summer and fall, Josiah, William, and Ezekiel had followed their sisters all over Salem Village and Ipswich County, trying to discover where the girls always disappeared to in those rare free hours children had in Massachusetts in 1689. And all through the bleak, icy winter when it was impossible for anyone to venture into the woods, Josiah had listened while Ezekiel and William plotted and planned in the loft of the Hutchinson barn just how they would trail their sisters when the snow melted. But today the girls had surprised Josiah by slipping off right after dinner.

"There should be early wild strawberries upriver," their mother, Goodwife Hutchinson, had said to Hope. "I shall clear the table. You take a pail and see what you can find."

Josiah had seen the gleam in his sister's brown eyes and known she had a plan. And as he'd volunteered to search for the calf that had wandered off that morning, he'd felt the gleam in his own blue eyes and hoped no one had seen.

"Please do," his mother said. "It would please your father if you'd find her. But hurry back. We need wood for supper."

Moments later, from the west pasture, Josiah had watched Hope gather up her skirts and pail and run, as no young Puritan lady was supposed to. She didn't go upriver for strawberries, but headed straight in the direction of the Porter farm. With no time to get William and Ezekiel, Josiah had dashed alone to the muddy spot on the riverbank and waited.

That much they had figured out last fall, that the girls always headed somewhere in this area. But at the Ipswich River they always lost them in the thick trees.

Now with the buds just appearing on the winter-naked branches, Josiah could still make out the three retreating figures, his sister's dark curls taking the lead. They had taken the time to run up this side of the bank and pick their way across on the rocks upstream.

If I cross here, Josiah thought, *I can make up time on the other side and maybe even get up a tree before they see me.*

His hands shaking with excitement, Josiah pulled off his leather boots and woolen stockings and looked around for a place to hide them. They were important boots—he'd have to come back for them—but for now there was no time to waste.

He tucked them into the underbrush, rolled his already short breeches above his knees, and then ran as fast as he could. His leather pouch bounced against his thigh. It always carried his wooden whistle in case he had to signal William or Ezekiel.

The mud sucked at his bare feet. If he wasn't so anxious to find the girls' secret hiding place, he would love to stop to enjoy the oozing between his toes. It had been a long winter in clunky boots.

Josiah stopped for a moment at the water's edge and strained to see upstream. The white caps had turned to tiny specks in the distance. Josiah plunged his feet into the river. The water was icy and his toes were numb before he took two steps. He and his friends had walked across the Ipswich here a hundred times a summer when there was more time to get away and explore the outskirts of the village. He had never tried crossing in spring—there was always the planting to help with and stray calves to find.

A tiny lap of guilt licked at Josiah's insides, but he tried to concentrate on the water rushing between his ankles. It never moved this fast in summer, and it never seemed so deep at this point.

The girls were getting farther away by the second. Josiah leaned forward, pushing his legs against the cold current as he moved toward the opposite bank. Maybe if he headed upstream a little as he crossed, he could save some time.

Holding his arms up to keep his sleeves dry, Josiah slanted his body and charged for shore. Suddenly the water surged around his waist and then immediately cupped into his armpits. Josiah splashed his hand out for a branch that stuck out from the bank, but it broke off in his hand, and he felt his feet leave the river bottom. He fought madly toward land, but the freezing water, free from the icy prison of winter, swept him downstream.

Although Josiah flailed his arms and kicked his legs, the river was boss. A Puritan never let the water completely cover his body, so learning to swim was out of the question. It was against the rules of the church. And even if he could swim, he could never overcome this swirling river.

"Help me!" Josiah screamed. But only the black water answered; like a powerful hand, it filled his mouth and pulled him under.

He came up choking and sputtering, and as he tried to scream again, another yank grabbed at him and pulled him back under. It was harder to splash now, harder to kick for the surface. Josiah climbed hard toward the sun sparkling at the top, but he only seemed to sink further.

God—help me! I can't breathe—please, Lord—I can't breathe!

And then a pair of fingers seemed to fold around Josiah's arms, pulling him up and up.

Up—

Josiah went limp, and the last thought curled through. *I'm going up. I see the sun.*

With a tearing, choking gasp of air he was above the water and just before the world went black he felt the arms around him.

Fading in his eyes was the brown face of an Indian boy.

✝ ⸭ ✝

Chapter Two

This squirrel you've brought me, Oneko—it may be the largest I've ever seen! Put him here by the fire."

Someone has gone squirrel hunting, Josiah thought. *I know how to skin them myself.*

"Yes, Oneko—a very large squirrel indeed. Hello there, lad—can you hear me?"

Josiah felt the warmth of hearthstones through his wet back, and his eyes sprang open. Looking into them were a pair as blue as his own, sparkling out of an elfin face.

"Hello, Big Squirrel," said the woman.

Josiah struggled to sit up, but two pairs of hands held him back, her gnarled ones, and the brown ones belonging to the Indian boy. Josiah shrank back in terror.

"He won't hurt you, lad," said the woman in her pleasantly raspy voice. "Oneko is just a boy himself. He won't hurt you— he saved your life."

It all rushed back to him, just as the water had rushed over his head and left him floundering like a baby in the river. A hot flush crept up Josiah's face.

"Thanks," he mumbled.

To his surprise, the Indian boy nodded solemnly.

"That means 'you are welcome,'" the elf woman said.

"Can he speak English?" Josiah asked.

"He understands what we say, though I still can't get him to answer. But we communicate—we manage."

Oneko looked from one to the other with interested eyes. Josiah had always thought Indian children were born with tiny tomahawks in their hands, ready to slit the throats of neighboring children. Oneko's eyes were alive and curious, not threatening. Still, Josiah sat up on the hearth and pulled his wet legs against him. It wouldn't hurt to be careful.

"So you've had a swim, have you?" the elf woman said.

"I didn't mean to!" Josiah said. "I was—on the bank—and suddenly—I was in the water!" He ducked his head. He always knew what he was thinking, but it was sometimes hard to get those thoughts to come out of his mouth. Whenever he sputtered, his sister laughed and called him a brainless boy.

"Oneko doesn't seem to think that's exactly how it happened." The elf woman's eyes sparkled merrily.

Josiah looked at the Indian whose eyes crinkled with silent laughter. Josiah ducked his head again.

"It doesn't matter," the woman said. "What matters is that you're safe. Let's get you out of those wet clothes, eh?"

She took off her big shawl and spread it in front of the fire to warm it. "I shall go for more wood. It will take some doing to dry those things. Out of them now!"

Before Josiah could protest, she'd slipped easily out the door and he was left—with the savage. That's what they called Indians in Salem Village, where they were shot on sight before they could steal babies or burn down houses. Many farmers even carried guns in their fields where they were easy prey for savages who skulked through the woods.

Oneko stood up, and Josiah, too, scrambled to his feet. Now that the elf woman was gone, the Indian might show his true colors and pull out a weapon—

But the savage held out his bare hand.

"What?" Josiah said, his voice shaking. Stories he'd heard over and over of good Christian people who were brutally slain by the Indians marched through his brain like a parade of demons.

Oneko touched his hand lightly against Josiah's soaked shirt. Josiah stiffened.

"What?" he said again.

Oneko tugged at his own leathery vest-like shirt, then pointed to the white cloth that stuck to Josiah's skin.

"Oh." Josiah shrugged sheepishly. "You mean—you're saying take it off—take the shirt off?"

Oneko patiently held out his hand.

Josiah peeled off his clothes and his pouch in three fast peels and wrapped himself quickly in the warm shawl. "I knew—I knew that—that was what you meant," he said.

Oneko didn't smile, but his eyes danced. He picked up the whistle pouch and toyed with it while Josiah watched him nervously.

"Friends now, I see." The elf woman left the door open to the spring breeze and crossed the room with an armload of wood. Oneko dropped the pouch and held out his arms for it, and she wiped her hands on her apron.

"Then it's time we became friends as well," she said. "My name is Faith, by God's will, and Hooker, by my husband's." She chuckled almost to herself. "I'm proud to be the Widow Hooker. It's a title I would challenge the queen herself for." She raised her eyebrows. "And you are?"

"Josiah. Josiah Hutchinson. My father is—"

"I know who your father is. Joseph Hutchinson, a man of excellent reputation in Salem Village." Josiah thought he saw a shadow pass through her eyes. "A godly man, among many who are not."

As quickly as the shadow appeared it faded, and Josiah found himself studying the merriest face he'd seen in his 10 years. It was small like the rest of her and shaped like a diamond. The blue eyes that had sparkled at him when he'd awakened were surrounded by a web of tiny wrinkles that creased and uncreased happily as she talked. Like the Puritan women he knew, his mother and Elizabeth Proctor and Prudence Porter, she wore her hair tucked away from her face. But no cap covered it, and the white knot of hair shone in the light of the fire as she hung a kettle of water over its flames. A few wispy whiskers sprouted impishly from her tiny chin, and Josiah watched them as she talked and worked.

"You are some ways from home, then, Josiah Hutchinson," she said. "As soon as we have dried these clothes and fed you, we had best find a way to get you back, eh? Your mother will have supper waitin'." She nodded toward Oneko who was spreading Josiah's shirt and breeches on the hearth. "Oneko can take you as far as Peter's Meadow. I am sure you can find your way from there, eh?"

"Peter's Meadow!" Josiah gasped. "But what—where—where are we?"

"Topsfield," the Widow Hooker said. "Just on the north edge of Blind Hole Meadow. But not to worry. None of the silly stories about the Blind Hole are true." The wrinkles seemed to crackle with delight. "I have never lost a visitor there yet."

That wasn't what worried Josiah. What set the tongues of fear to lapping at his insides was that he was miles from home—probably farther than he had ever been on foot—or certainly on Indian back. It was definitely the farthest he'd ever been without his father. It would be almost dark before his clothes were dry, and well into evening before he reached the Hutchinson house in Salem Village—without the stray calf, with no wood chopped for the supper fire, without the pigs fed . . .

"The season's first strawberries." The Widow Hooker placed a blue bowl on the table, the only large piece of furniture in the tiny room. She chuckled. "I sent my friend off for strawberries and he brought me a Big Squirrel, too. Come to the table, my friends."

Josiah tried not to stare at Oneko as he pulled up a stool to the Widow Hooker's table. He had always imagined that the Indians squatted by their fires and devoured uncooked animal parts with their bare hands. Oneko ate the berries and cream with a spoon, and his bread disappeared into his mouth without a crumb left on the table.

"You're hungry, Oneko," the Widow Hooker said. "As well you should be, carrying this prize all the way from Log Bridge."

Josiah looked up sharply.

"Log Bridge." She nodded. "Someday you must tell us what you were doing in the Ipswich River, Josiah. It will make quite a story, I'm sure."

Oneko made a grunting noise, and his eyes flickered playfully at Josiah.

The widow went on, talking about a blue jay, Mrs. Jay, she called her, who squawked every morning as she hustled around gathering building supplies, and about the squirrels who had beaten her to the nearby berries.

"I am lucky to have Oneko," she said, "or I would have to give my cream to the squirrel family and say, 'Enjoy.'"

Does Oneko live here with you? Josiah wanted to ask. *Don't you have to kill the animals for food, the way we do? How do you live with no husband and no farm?*

But as quickly as the questions crowded into his mind they were nudged out by the happy talk that trickled through the afternoon. The shadows were long on the wall when Oneko grunted from the fire—which meant that Josiah's clothes were dry, and it was time to make the trek south to Salem Village.

"Now I see a pair of breeches and a shirt that a mother might not frown at," the Widow Hooker said when Josiah was dressed. "But there is the matter of stockings—and boots . . . "

Her voice trailed off, and Josiah stared in a panic at his bare feet.

"It could be a long walk, what with the mud and the

brambles," she said. "Oneko can, of course, carry you to Peter's Meadow, but from there—"

Josiah could walk from Salem Village to Boston in bare feet. But the look on his father's face when he came home without his boots was a sight Josiah did not want to see.

The day his father gave them to him was carved in Josiah's mind for all time. Josiah was in the hayloft a few days before that, pitching hay down to the oxen. The straw dotted the barn floor in big tufts that invited Josiah to jump down into one, just once. He leaped from the loft and fell straight through a pile of hay, jamming his foot into a nail on the floor. It poked right through the soft sole of his moccasin and left a gaping hole in his heel. Dr. Griggs was called in and Josiah couldn't walk—or do any of his chores—for a week.

During that time, his father came up to his room and dropped a pair of heavy leather boots on the floor by his bed.

"As soon as you are able to walk, you are to put these on." The lines in his father's face were tired and he'd sighed. "They are men's boots, and you are not fit to wear them yet. But you are my only son. I must have your help or I cannot run this farm. Perhaps when you wear them they will remind you to think, and you won't do such foolish things."

And then he'd shaken his head as if he doubted that could ever happen.

Josiah's mouth went dry now. Leaving those boots who knows where was probably the most brainless thing he'd done yet. Even if he could remember where he'd left them, someone had probably carried them off by now—

The Widow Hooker chuckled softly, as if she had read

Josiah's mind. He looked up—and saw his boots waiting in the doorway, the stockings tucked neatly into the tops.

"Where—!"

"Oneko—you are the master of secrets," the widow said.

Oneko slid silently into the doorway, and his eyes met Josiah's.

"A safe journey to you both," the widow said when Josiah was at last fully dressed.

Josiah stepped outside into the dusk, and the responsibility he had left behind him when he was carried into the cabin flooded over him. He remembered his manners.

"I shall tell my mother of your kindness," Josiah said to the Widow Hooker.

Her diamond eyes clouded. "It would be best to keep my kindness to yourself," she said quietly. "Your mother and father would not be pleased to know that you were here."

"But why?" Josiah cried.

"If they ask, of course, you mustn't lie." She swept the clouds from her eyes and smiled at Oneko. "Take care of our Big Squirrel. And God be with you."

Oneko took off without a sound into the gathering darkness. Josiah followed, and when he turned to look back, the door to the cabin was closed.

✠ ⊹ ✠

ou know, people—my people, that is—say that men have crossed Blind Hole Meadow and—and are never—I mean to say—they just disappear. No one even finds—finds their—you know—their bodies."

Oneko looked back at Josiah, shook his head, and continued to plunge through the darkness at a pace Josiah could barely keep up with.

"It is true! That *is* what people say—"

Josiah's voice trailed off. He usually didn't say much. The words always got tangled up and came out in knots. He was only talking now to keep the nagging thoughts out of his mind. The ones that said, *You are in a great deal of trouble, Mister. You would be wise to be prayin' to the Good Lord now that your father hasn't already gone out lookin' for you.*

Josiah shook his head and talked on. "People are always believing in silly stories around here. I don't believe—"

15

In front of him, Oneko stopped abruptly, and Josiah nearly ran up the backs of his legs.

"What?" Josiah said.

Oneko pointed into the gentle valley formed by the hill they were standing on.

"This is Misty Hill, then!" Josiah said.

Oneko nodded.

Below a few flickering lights winked through windows, of the Osborns' house to one side, Josiah guessed, and Captain John Putnam's to the other. Josiah felt a pang in his stomach. He was in enough trouble. He certainly didn't want to meet up with any of the Putnams on his way home.

"That would be Thorndike Hill there, aye?" he said to Oneko.

The Indian boy grunted softly. Josiah searched in the darkness for his two-story gray clapboard house.

"Our farm is—is just to the other side of it. You see—?"

But Oneko had slipped away into the night.

Josiah tried to open the heavy front door without a sound. He crossed the narrow stone-floored hallway and stood inside the kitchen, then realized that every eye was on him, as if his family were staring at the doorway all afternoon, waiting for his return.

Goody Hutchinson closed her eyes, and Josiah knew she was giving thanks that he was safe. He swallowed hard.

Hope tilted her chin. *We girls won again,* her eyes said. She faced the fire to hide the smile Josiah saw playing at the corners of her mouth.

Forcing his head to turn, Josiah looked finally at his father. Joseph Hutchinson sat by the smokey rush lamp, not moving.

A book lay open in his lap, and his hands gripped the arms of the chair. They were big hands, rough and cracked from hard work. Work Josiah had not helped with that day. The happy hours at the Widow Hooker's slipped out of his mind, and Josiah stared down at his boots, now caked with telltale mud.

"So, you've come home, have you?" his father said.

"Aye, sir," Josiah answered.

"And have you found the stray calf?"

"No, sir."

Josiah's father slapped the book shut and dropped it on the table with a thud. "What are your duties as a son?"

Josiah's eyes searched the room wildly for help. His mother sat beside his father, looking at her lap. Hope's back was to him as she worked at the fire, but Josiah could imagine her eyes laughing.

"What are they?" his father repeated.

"To honor my father and—and—my mother," Josiah said.

"Aye. Go on."

"And to help them in the running of the farm—and not to bring shame on the family."

"And is that what you have done today?"

The lump in Josiah's throat was so large he couldn't answer. He shook his head slowly.

"I cannot hear you," his father said.

"I did not—I didn't—I didn't help," Josiah managed to say. "And I disobeyed you."

"Deceived us, aye?"

"Aye. But I have brought no shame on the family."

"Except that your mother was seen by Captain Walcott

bringin' in wood for her own supper fire, when he and every-one else in Salem Village knows she has a fine big son to do that work for her."

Josiah didn't care what Captain John Walcott thought, and he knew his father didn't, either. Walcott was a friend of the Putnams, who were no friends of the Hutchinsons. But he did care what his mother thought.

"For—forgive me," Josiah said to her.

"Aye," she said softly.

"I think you had best be asking God to forgive you now," his father said. "You have caused this family a pile of worryin' this day."

His chair scraped the plank floor as he got up, and Josiah shrank back. Slowly his father came toward him, and even more slowly his hand went around Josiah's arm. Josiah closed his eyes. *Just do it quickly,* he thought. *Just whip me and let's be done with it.*

But as slowly as he'd taken hold of him, his father let him go. Josiah sneaked a glance at him.

"You'd best be upstairs and on your knees," Papa said. "Tomorrow you'll see me before the sun comes up. You have some makin' up to do for today."

Joseph Hutchinson's piercing blue eyes remained steady under the thick sandy eyebrows that matched his hair, hair like Josiah's. They looked inside Josiah and came out *knowing things,* Josiah thought.

"Be gone with you!" he said.

And Josiah was—but not before he saw Hope turn her head sharply from the fire, protest in her eyes.

He climbed the narrow winding stairs and reached his and Hope's room, which was separated from his parents' bedroom by a sitting room. He slipped into his nightshirt and knelt next to his bed. As he rested his head against the bed, he felt the ropes that held up the mattress, and his thoughts ran. *I want the light of God. I want the sweet love of Jesus. Forgive me for my—boots—and strawberries and cream—I am a Big Squirrel, Oneko.*

"You are a big, brainless boy," a voice whispered in his ear. "Get into bed before you get that whipping after all."

Josiah woke with a start. "You would like to see that, wouldn't you?" he said sleepily to his sister as she shoved him onto his soft feather mattress.

"I'm content already." Hope climbed into her own bed on the other side of the room and wriggled down under the eiderdown quilt. "You followed us—I know you did—but you did not find us. When will you learn that you just aren't as smart as I am?"

Wide awake now, Josiah propped himself up on one elbow on the bed cushions. "Why do you suppose Papa didn't whip me?"

"Quiet," she said. "I'm praying that he will come to his senses and do it anyway."

He knew Hope didn't pray for long. Within a few minutes, her breathing became heavy as she drifted off behind the hangings that curtained her bed. Puritan children worked hard, and sleep was always there when their heads touched their bed cushions at night.

But in spite of Josiah's busy day, his mind was far from sleep. Quietly, he padded to the window and settled himself on top of the trunk that held the heavy winter clothes and blankets they had just packed away. Although it was spring, a chill hung in the night air, and Josiah pulled his knees to his chest as he peered through the diamond-shaped panes to the farm below.

His mind had been so busy since he'd left the Widow Hooker's, he hadn't had time to go back and look at the day in his memory as he liked to do. Things crowded a person's mind so much when they were happening, Josiah always liked to go back later and take them out to look them over and see what they were really made of.

He held many things in his mind tonight that he could bring out and enjoy again—the warm glow of that bare, clean room, the strawberries that never tasted better, being saved from drowning in the Ipswich River, sitting in a room with an *Indian*, and being named the Big Squirrel by the widow.

The Widow Hooker. She was so different from his mother and Goodwife Proctor and Goodwife Porter. They were good, quiet women who always knew just what to do next. Godly women, they were called. They were too busy to spend a whole afternoon with two boys, and one of them an Indian. They would be called crazy or perhaps even put in stocks in front of the Meeting House. But the Widow Hooker seemed to have nothing to do but to talk and watch the wild animals and befriend an Indian boy.

Perhaps that was why she told him not to tell anyone about her—especially his parents. What would they really think if they knew he'd met a woman who, with full knowledge of his foolishness, helped him dry his clothes, fed him, and sent him on his way back home? And above all this, claimed to be God-fearing?

Josiah was about to chase that thought through his brain when his eye caught something below. He got up on his knees and pressed his face to the glass.

There it was again—a shadow at the far corner of the farm where it touched the road. It was late, later than most hardworking Puritans would be out and about. Silently, he swung the window open and leaned forward to squint into the night.

Two figures hurried by on the road. They were men, he could tell, and their faces were turned toward the ground. They stopped and nodded to each other. Then the taller one hurried off into the night. Josiah scanned the road. The nearest house in that direction belonged to Nathaniel Putnam, one of his father's archenemies. The next house, past theirs, was that of the Reverend Samuel Parris. The other, smaller man went that way.

Why would Reverend Parris be coming from the Putnams' place late on the evening before the Sabbath? And why—

Josiah shook his head. Too many mysteries for a boy who had to waken before sunrise to do some "makin' up." Suddenly, his bones ached and the lids sagged over his blue eyes. He was asleep almost before he reached his bed.

✢ ✢ ✢

Chapter Four

By the time Josiah had chopped and brought in enough wood for the day, fed the pigs, chickens, and turkeys, watered the horses, and gathered the eggs, the sun had come up over Salem Village. As he stumbled to breakfast, he almost wished his father had decided on a whipping instead. He always had chores, but usually they were spread out from morning to evening. He'd never before done them all before the light of day.

His parents, he knew, would be upstairs dressing for Sunday Meeting. He'd expected to have to get his own meal this morning—part of the "makin' up." So he was surprised to find Hope in the kitchen, stirring the brass pot that hung on the trammel. She was already dressed in the dove-colored dress she would wear to Meeting; it was covered by an apron.

"Breakfast?" she said sharply, her voice even huskier than usual.

"Aye. But why are *you* serving it?"

She didn't answer, but noisily dropped a wooden trencher of cornbread and butter on the table in front of him.

Josiah stared at it. "Thanks."

"Hold your tongue!" she said through her teeth and plunked a pewter mug next to the plate. Springwater splashed out and over his hand.

After a quick prayer of thanks, he chewed thoughtfully and watched Hope scrape his parents' trenchers with sand to clean them.

"But why are you—" he started.

"If you *must* be a party to everyone else's affairs—" Her eyes snapped as she whirled toward him. "I, too, am being punished for coming home yesterday—" She stopped, and her always-red cheeks turned cherry-colored.

Josiah tingled. "Yes?"

"With the bottom of my skirts wet."

"From your—from your journey up the Ipswich River!" Josiah cried happily. "You should have held your skirts up higher."

Hope's eyes blazed. "You brainless—"

"You said I didn't—couldn't—that I couldn't find you."

"All right then, where were we going?"

Josiah shrugged and stuffed the rest of his cornbread into his mouth. Hope sniffed importantly and turned back to the fire.

They hadn't always been enemies. They had once spent all their rare free hours together, blowing soap bubbles on the breeze in spring, playing cat's cradle with cords in front of the fire in winter. He remembered summer days when they'd dammed up a rivulet in a stream with a tile and made boats to float on the tiny pool. He was silent until he was nearly four, and Hope was always the one to tell their mother what he wanted. Two years older, she had eventually taught him how to talk.

But sometime last year, just before Hope turned 12, she began to prefer the company of Rachel Porter and Sarah Proctor. That wouldn't have bothered Josiah so much—he had Ezekiel and William to sled and carve wooden whistles with—but she had begun to behave as if she were somehow above him: smarter, wittier, and better at everything. She was always tilting her chin or tossing her dark curls in a way that made Josiah want to be smarter, wittier, and better at everything. He was sure he never would be. He'd heard people say she was the "bright one." About him they said nothing except to ask why he stammered and stuttered when he talked.

So when Ezekiel and William had shared the same complaints about their sisters, the game of uncovering the girls' secrets had begun. Yesterday he was so close—

"Oh! Ouch!" Hope shook her finger, then stuck it angrily into her mouth.

"What?" Josiah said.

"I'm burned all over from these pots!" She whipped around to face him. "Have you had enough?"

"Of what?"

"Of your breakfast!"

Josiah nodded. The flare of her anger could send him into silence faster than anything.

"It would be a cold day in Barbados before you would see Abigail Williams and Betty Parris slaving over a fire, serving some boy his breakfast!" she went on.

"Where's Barbados?" Josiah asked timidly.

"It's an island somewhere, where it never snows and everyone has servants to do their work for them—just like the Reverend Parris does. And then his daughter and his niece lie in bed until their Barbados slave Tituba lays out their Sunday clothes—and churns their butter—and weeds their gardens—agh!"

Hope yanked off her apron and hung it on its peg.

"That's why you hate Abigail Williams so much," Josiah said.

"Hate is a strong word, Josiah," she said primly, sounding like the Reverend Parris himself. "And that isn't why I dislike her—" Hope stopped pacing for a minute and seemed to forget Josiah was there as she talked into the air. "She lies. And I've seen her laughing during Meeting—during prayers! Watch today and see if you don't catch her at it."

Her eyes met Josiah's, and for a moment, there was a feeling of partnership. It faded as Hope turned to go.

"Papa doesn't like Reverend Parris, either," Josiah said. "Maybe it isn't a sin to—not to like his niece."

"Be ready to walk to Meeting by eight," she said in reply. "I was to tell you. It's an important Sabbath for Mama and Papa."

The Meeting House was only a five-minute walk from the Hutchinsons' farm, which was sad to Josiah because the walk was the only part of Sunday he liked. The drummer would march up and down the road tapping out the rhythm that called them to Meeting. They had to pass the pillory and whipping post and stocks, where Josiah imagined the constables, Willard and Cheever, hauling men in for the punishment of some wicked, delicious crime.

"Stand aside now," Papa said suddenly.

Josiah heard the thundering of hoofbeats and, without looking up, knew the Putnams were arriving. There were 20 of them, brothers and their sons, and the cloud of dust they raised as their horses danced and strutted down the road in front of the Meeting House set everyone to coughing.

"Those Putnams are awfully proud of the way they ride," Josiah's father muttered.

Josiah had to admit they were the best riders in Essex County, and he secretly liked watching their horses prance in place as they were tied to the hitching posts. But all too soon he had to leave the spring sunshine and go into the stark interior of the square, brown Meeting House.

At least in the spring, the gallery loft where Josiah, Ezekiel, William, and the other boys crowded in for the Meeting was neither steamy with heat nor icy with cold. But no matter what the season, the benches were hard and the Reverend Parris's sermons long, and until fall there would be no dried pumpkin seeds to spit at their sisters below. Josiah found William and Ezekiel and squeezed between them at the back of the loft.

"What became of you yesterday?" towheaded William Proctor whispered in Josiah's ear.

"Hope came to our place lookin' for you," Ezekiel Porter hissed from the other side. "We thought you'd been taken by Indians!" His enormous hazel eyes scanned the gallery for Deacon Edward Putnam, the tithing man, and his pole. They'd be poked soundly if they were caught talking.

"I *was* taken by Indians—one Indian," Josiah said out of a tiny hole he made with the side of his mouth.

Ezekiel and William squealed, then clapped their hands over their mouths. The deacon appeared from nowhere, carrying his stick with its knob on one end and dangling foxtail on the other. The tail was for tickling the faces of any adults who fell asleep during the sermon. The knob was for tapping mischievous boys on the head. The deacon swung it in their direction now in warning fashion.

Too far away for a poke, Josiah thought. But for safety's sake, all three boys folded their hands in their laps. Josiah stole a look at the benches below.

He knew his parents would sit on opposite sides of the church, and Hope would sit properly with their mother and the other women on the east side. Josiah craned his neck toward Mrs. Parris's place to find Abigail.

As he gazed, his eye caught his father approaching his usual spot on a bench on the men's west side. But it was already occupied—by Nathaniel Putnam.

The Putnams never sat near the Hutchinsons or Porters or Proctors. There were "unsettled differences" between them, Josiah's father always said, so they all coolly avoided each other on the Sabbath. But now it seemed as if Nathaniel Putnam were sitting in his father's seat on purpose, as if he were waiting for Joseph Hutchinson to challenge him.

The whole church seemed to hold its breath. Solemnly, Josiah's father nodded to Nathaniel, sat down next to him and bowed his head. Slowly, like a man escaping the fangs of a snake, Nathaniel Putnam slid away from Joseph Hutchinson and hunched his shoulders in disgust.

Half the church gasped while the other half pulled away like baking bread from the sides of a pan. Josiah's eyes darted to his mother on the other side of the Meeting House. Putnam women sat in a rigid row behind her, sniffing the air as if Mama were the source of some terrible odor.

Josiah's thoughts raced. *Why? Why were the Putnams and others being cruel to his parents? Right here in the Lord's house!*

A deep silence settled over the church, and everyone stood as Reverend Parris stepped to the front.

Josiah leaned forward suddenly. *What would he look like in the dark, hurrying along the road with his head down?*

Today Reverend Parris looked as he always did—slender, perfectly dressed in black, and pinched.

Pinched was the word Josiah had used in his mind to describe their minister ever since he had come to Salem Village six months before, in November. Until then there was no real church in Salem Village—only in Salem Town. When Reverend Parris agreed to answer the call of the village people to be their minister, the church was officially formed. And the Reverend Parris had promised that a new age would dawn in Salem Village now that they had a covenanted church. The community could now be peaceful and united. But people like his father were bothered by the many things Reverend Parris asked for before he accepted the job. He wanted the people of the church to provide him with firewood and give him the deed to the home he would live in. But the promise of peace in the Society of the Church was exciting to everyone, even the children. His father had agreed to give the new preacher a chance.

Reverend Parris, however, had not seemed excited at all. He never seemed excited about anything, actually. He just seemed pinched—pinched cheeks, squinting pinched glare, puckered and pinched mouth. *Knowing the Lord doesn't make him happy,* Josiah always thought. *He looks like a dried-up turkey about to go under the hatchet.*

The second deacon, Deacon Walcott, stepped to the front, opened the Bay Psalm Book, and sang the first line of the psalm. Josiah moved his mouth, as if to answer with the rest of the congregation, but his eyes wandered about the church. When they lit on the table next to Reverend Parris, his heart skipped a beat.

On the table were a loaf of bread, covered with a snowy white cloth, and a pitcher that gleamed in the one ray of sun that managed to filter through the narrow window behind it. This, Josiah remembered, was to be their first communion in the Church of Christ in Salem Village. Today, they would learn who the new covenanted members of the church were.

Josiah remembered previous Sabbaths, when those who wished to become covenanted members came forward and were questioned by those who were already members—the handful who were elected when Reverend Parris first arrived.

Each person had to reveal the experience with God that led him or her to believe he was one of God's chosen. Josiah preferred their stories to the frightening tales Reverend Parris told in his sermons about the torment awaiting all unsaved sinners.

Josiah—and even Hope—liked their parents' stories the most. If any people were good enough to be members of God's church, Joseph and Deborah Hutchinson were among them.

Today it would be announced. Josiah forgot Abigail and even the Putnams and their friends who made a wide, empty circle around the Hutchinsons. He swung his legs in excitement as the congregation was seated.

After the opening prayer, the deacon turned over the hourglass and sat on the deacon's bench in front of the pulpit as Reverend Parris began his sermon. This was usually the time the boys made faces at the backs of their sisters' heads or saw how many times they could force the deacon to wave his stick in warning against things he hadn't really seen them do.

Josiah loved the Bible. He wasn't allowed to touch it until he was able to read it, and with little schooling in Salem Village, that was like a distant dream. But he liked the way his father read it to them morning and night, and the way he prayed in the evenings and at meals, as if God were perhaps right there among them. But with Reverend Parris, it was different. In the Meeting House, God seemed far away and so Josiah usually drifted, too.

But today he craned forward to listen. Somewhere in the sermon, Reverend Parris would reveal the names of those who were elected by the members to join their ranks.

The deacon turned the hourglass twice before the minister cleared his throat for the list. Josiah felt the congregation leaning, waiting.

"When I have completed the reading of the list," Reverend Parris said in his pinched voice, "covenanted members old and new—the visible saints of our faith—will stay to eat and drink in memory of our Lord's last supper and passion. The rest of the congregation will, of course, leave and return after the noon meal."

A current of excitement shot up Josiah's spine. He and Hope would have to leave. They couldn't become covenanted members themselves until they were old enough to have an experience that made them worthy. But it was a thrill to think of his parents partaking of the Lord's supper in their own church in their own town. It meant they were part of what he had heard his father talk of many times: living witnesses to the power of God.

Reverend Parris began to read. "Nathaniel Ingersoll. Nathaniel Putnam. John Putnam—"

Josiah stiffened, but he strained to listen to Reverend Parris.

"Thomas Flint—"

Reverend Parris read 26 names in all. When he was finished, the names of John Proctor, Joseph Porter, and Joseph Hutchinson were not among them. None of their wives were listed, either.

Josiah blinked. Maybe he was trying so hard to concentrate he'd missed them. But one look at the scene below told him

that wasn't true. Hope and her mother had their chins tilted
as far up as they would go, and the broad shoulders of Joseph
Hutchinson were stony still in his black waistcoat. Josiah
blinked hard again to hold back the tears.

"Let us bow our heads in prayer," Reverend Parris said.

Josiah doubted that much praying was going on in the
Proctor, Porter, and Hutchinson rows. Even Ezekiel and
William had their fists doubled instead of their hands folded.

Almost before the "Amen" sounded and the doors were
opened to let nonmembers out, Josiah's father was gone from
the Meeting House. Josiah scrambled down the stairs and
squeezed between a sea of black skirts.

"Watch it, boy!" said a voice just above his head.

Josiah looked into the green, narrow eyes of Abigail
Williams, the Reverend Parris's niece. At the moment, Josiah
didn't care whether she laughed in church or had breakfast in
bed. He only wanted to get to his father.

William's and Ezekiel's fathers stood in a somber knot
with old Israel Porter, Ezekiel's grandfather, and Ezekiel's
handsome cousin Giles who was always at his grandfather's
side. His father would join them, and they would all bend
their heads and find a way to fix it.

But Joseph Hutchinson stood apart. His wife and daughter
were still working their way out of the Meeting House, and he
was alone—more alone than Josiah had ever seen him. His
powerful jaw was etched against the blue sky, and anger
seemed to singe even his brooding eyebrows. Josiah was
always cautious in his father's presence, careful about what he
said and did. But now, he was afraid.

"Come along, Josiah," his mother spoke softly from behind him.

Without a word, they joined his father and marched in a line away from the Meeting House.

"Joseph!" Goodman Proctor called after them. "We have all planned to meet at Ingersoll's Ordinary following the afternoon meeting. We must decide what's to be done about this!"

"I will never darken the door of Ingersoll's place again," Josiah's father answered. "And it's sure I won't be back for the afternoon meeting—or any other that takes place in this church. I will not be a part of this Society."

And turning on his heel, he led his family home.

✠ ⋅✠⋅ ✠

Chapter Five

*A*h, there you are, you ninny!"

The calf looked up from the brook and gave a pitiful bleat as Josiah slipped the loop of rope over her head.

"At least you had sense enough to find water," he said. "But your mother is near to burstin' with milk for you."

She licked the side of his face with her thick pink tongue and Josiah hugged her neck. Finding her was the only good thing that had happened all day.

"Come on, Ninny. That's what you're to be named. Ninny." He tugged gently on the rope and she pulled her feet out of Beaver Brook and followed him, bleating sadly every now and then.

"Oh, shut it," Josiah laughed. "You're going home to your mama. What more do you want?"

"Ble-e-eh."

Josiah led her across Wolf Pits Meadow toward home,

where she could nurse and where his father would have one less thing to worry about.

It was a strange day for the Hutchinsons. Usually the Sabbath was filled with a morning service, a noonday meal at Ingersoll's or a neighbor's or home, and an afternoon service that lasted, in the spring, until it was nearly dark.

But there would be no afternoon service at the Salem Village Church for them, today or ever, and so the Sabbath stretched on like a long, lazy road. No one worked on the Sabbath. Hope was sitting under a tree. His mother rested in the window of the best room, the room opposite the kitchen, which was saved for Sundays and special occasions.

His father. Josiah shivered a little. When he had last seen him, Josiah's father was standing at the west end of the farm, still as a post, staring toward Putnam land. Josiah could almost smell the thoughts burning inside Joseph Hutchinson's brain.

That was when he decided to do something to ease his father's burden, and he'd gone to look for the calf. She wasn't hard to find, with all the racket she was making in Beaver Brook. Jonathan Walcott could have heard her himself and brought her home—if he weren't a friend of the Putnams.

Until today, Josiah thought the trouble between the Putnam clan and the Hutchinsons, Porters, and Proctors, was about property or maybe stolen pigs. But today, in the Meeting House, he learned it was much more serious. You didn't refuse to allow another Puritan into the church family unless the hate went deep.

Hate is a strong word, Josiah, he could hear Hope saying.

He was afraid he was feeling some of that strong stuff right now.

Josiah reached the base of Thorndike Hill with Ninny still trailing behind. Deacon Walcott and Reverend Parris would return from Meeting any minute, and so Josiah steered the calf away from their houses. A vision of the men in the darkness, hurrying past their house last night, popped back into Josiah's mind. Had they discussed leaving his father and mother out of the membership right there on the road as he'd watched?

His thoughts were erased by the sound of shouting from the west end of the Hutchinsons' farm.

"Off my property, Putnam!" his father yelled.

The booming voice of Thomas Putnam burst back. "Not until I've had my say!"

"Ble-e-eh!" the calf cried.

Josiah pulled her into the trees. "Shhhh!" he whispered. "I must hear this."

"That sawmill of yours—" Thomas Putnam boomed.

"That sawmill of Israel Porter's!"

"Be straight with me, Hutchinson. You own half interest in it, do you not?"

"Aye—what business is it of yours?"

Josiah couldn't see their faces, but through the branches he saw that Thomas Putnam's neck was an angry purple. "That sawmill is flooding my property! That's what business it is of mine! That water is to be dammed up, or I'll slap a lawsuit on you, d'y'hear?"

"That is not your—"

"That *is* my land!" Thomas Putnam was close to exploding. "It stands clear in my grandfather's will—"

"Then he willed you land that never belonged to him," Goodman Hutchinson said. "Good day, Mr. Putnam."

Neither man moved. The butterflies flitting around them seemed to suspend in air for the moment. Only the bleating of Ninny brought the world to life again. Thomas Putnam spun around.

"You have your son spying for you now?" he cried.

Papa's great hooded eyes darted in Josiah's direction. Josiah sprang up and pulled Ninny out of the trees.

"I found her, sir," he stammered. "Over at Beaver Brook, she was. She'll need—the milk—the cow must be near to burstin' by now."

Thomas Putnam looked down at him, his lip curled.

"Then you'd best be takin' the calf to her, hadn't you?" The edge in Papa's voice sent Josiah off at a trot toward the pasture with Ninny in tow.

Ninny and her mother had a long, noisy argument before the nursing began. All parents were alike when it came to lost children, Josiah decided. Glumly, he sank to the ground. He'd made his father look foolish in front of Thomas Putnam. And he'd only wanted to make up for yesterday.

"Josiah."

Josiah turned to see his father leaning on the fence behind him, the anger still on his face.

Josiah scrambled up.

Joseph Hutchinson studied his son's face until Josiah finally looked at the ground. Those eyes did go inside and see

things, and at the moment Josiah didn't want him to see any
of it.

"Do you think, Josiah?" he said finally.

Josiah shifted uneasily. "Think? About—"

"About what you do—before you go about doing it? Before
draggin' a calf through the trees like a bumbling fool!"

"Aye—nay—"

"It's time you learned. These are changing times. You
cannot be foolish in these times. I've a mind to teach you the
work I do, and see if then—"

He stopped and stared hard at Josiah who waited for the
arm to come up and smack him.

"You understand what happened to us in the Meeting this
morning?" Papa asked suddenly.

Josiah blinked. "Aye. You aren't allowed—the members of
the church will not let you—because—"

"Because of hate."

Josiah sucked in a breath.

"Don't mistake me. The Putnams and others hate us. I
don't hate them or anyone else. But I do see through them—
and I do not like what I see."

It was almost as if he were telling himself, not Josiah. He
was quiet for a moment now, and Josiah held his breath.
*Should I tell him about Reverend Parris and his secret
meeting?* he thought.

His father pounded the top of the fence softly with his fist
and backed away.

"I must go to Israel Porter—we have much to discuss. Use
your time wisely today, for tomorrow you'll have little of it.

Tomorrow I will add more responsibilities to your—" He didn't
finish but walked toward the house. "Remember what I've said
to you."

"Aye," Josiah said to his father's back. *I don't know what
it means, but I'll remember it.*

Use your time wisely—that was the one he did understand. Josiah glanced anxiously at the sky and took off toward
Thorndike Hill at a gallop. If he ran hard enough, he could be
at the Widow Hooker's in a flash.

✛ ⬥ ✛

Chapter Six

ig Squirrel!" The Widow Hooker met Josiah at the door of the cabin. "You look as if you've run all the way from Boston, eh?"

Josiah could only nod. He was breathing too hard to speak, and in spite of the nip in the spring air, sweat rolled from the yellow curls around his ears.

"Your near-drownin' yesterday did you no harm, I see. Good. I haven't time to nurse you to health today. I have other patients." She turned abruptly and went in.

Unlike the day before, it was dark inside except for the fire. Blankets hung at both windows.

"Why have you made it so dark?" Josiah asked.

"Hush! They need quiet!"

"Who?" Josiah whispered.

She beckoned him to a wooden box on the hearth. From inside someone, or something, was screeching out a whine that outdid the deacon.

"What—"

"Shhh! Look!"

Josiah pulled back the widow's shawl that covered the box and peeked in. Inside, a rabbit breathed as if *she* had just run across Blind Hole Meadow.

"Is *she* makin' all that racket?" Josiah whispered.

The Widow Hooker nodded and stroked the long gray ears. "Well, then, shall we try again, Mama?" she said to the rabbit.

"Is she—"

"She's having a bit of trouble delivering these babies, but with some help from us—"

"Us?"

"Look after that water I have boilin' there, would you?" the Widow Hooker said.

Josiah was all too glad to because the widow was putting her hands into the rabbit's box, and the next high-pitched screech reminded Josiah of Sarah Proctor whenever she saw a snake.

"Ah!" The Widow Hooker held up a gooey lump in bright red hands. "One of God's precious creatures!"

Josiah's stomach churned. "Is that a baby rabbit?"

"Aye, and more are comin'. Where is that water, boy?"

A few minutes later, the widow held out another lump. This one didn't squirm.

"Is it dead?" Josiah asked.

The widow chuckled. "You don't waste words, do you, lad? No, he's not dead. He's just having a bit of trouble getting started. Put some clean linen on the table, Big Squirrel."

Josiah spread a cloth on the table and watched with wide eyes as the widow poked her finger into the tiny rabbit's mouth and scooped. The bunny wiggled a little.

"Good, then. We've cleared his throat. Let's get his heart to beating now."

Tenderly, she rubbed the little chest. A moment later, the miniature feet began to kick, and the widow tucked him into the box.

Within 15 minutes, Mother Rabbit had five tiny, oozy, hairless lumps nuzzling at her belly. The Widow Hooker mixed springwater with Josiah's boiled water and washed her hands while he dared a glance into the box.

"I thought rabbits could have their babies—alone," he said.

"By God's will, aye. But this one came to me for help, and I was willing to oblige."

"She *came* to you?"

"Aye," she said simply. "Now, then, will you have a dish of tea?"

Before Josiah could answer, he had a steaming mug in front of him and the widow across from him, chuckling softly.

"Now, Josiah Hutchinson, tell me why you've come."

"Hate," Josiah said.

The cobweb of lines on the widow's face sprang apart. "You don't say much, but when you do, lad—"

"Why do people hate?"

Actually, he hadn't known that was why he'd run up Thorndike Hill and across Wolf Pits, Peter's, and Blind Hole Meadows to see her. His thoughts just popped from his mouth with lives of their own.

"You've come to the right place, Big Squirrel," she said. "I am an expert on hate."

"Do you hate anyone?"

"No. Not a soul. But plenty of folks hate me."

The Widow Hooker got up and led Josiah out of the dark room into the sparkling spring sunlight. With mugs in hand they sat under an unruly-looking cherry tree whose blossoms were taking over the tiny yard. The Widow Hooker nestled a fallen one in her hand.

"About forty years ago," she began, "when I was a much younger girl, I met two men. One was Abraham Hooker. I married him. The other was George Fox. I believed in him."

She paused, as if that were the end of the story. Josiah stirred restlessly.

"Why did you—what did he say?"

"He said the Word of the Lord was so great, so powerful, that people should quake at the very sound of it. To tremble as the land does in an earthquake—not in fear so much as in awe, eh?"

Josiah nodded. He had trembled a number of times at the Reverend Parris's sermons.

"George Fox formed a group of people who believed as he did, and he called it the Society of Friends. Ah, Mr. Hooker and I, we were great members of that society. We dressed in plain dress and took on plain manners. Instead of all the singin' and swingin' of incense they were doin' in the Church of England, we took on simple ways of worshipin'." She chuckled softly. "We would sit for hours in silence because to talk would be to overshadow the Lord. It would have been a good life, except that the Church of England did not look kindly on our practices and tried to force us to worship as they did."

"Like the Puritans!" Josiah loved to hear his father tell the story of how his father, Josiah's grandfather, had brought his family to Massachusetts to escape the torture of the Church.

The same shadow Josiah had seen yesterday passed once again over the widow's face.

"It was indeed. All of God's children who couldn't serve their Lord as they wished longed for a place where they could worship freely. When we heard of the colonies here, we were sure we had found that place, and we came—Abraham Hooker and myself and many others. Seeking the freedom our hearts craved." Her voice drifted off and she fell silent.

"Didn't you find freedom?" Josiah asked.

The clouds on the widow's face grew dark, and Josiah was sorry he had asked. Slowly, she shook her head.

"You are a Puritan, are you not, Josiah?"

He nodded carefully.

"Then I cannot say anything against the godly people of your faith. And many of them *are* God's chosen."

There was another silence.

"Did something bad happen to you?" Josiah asked.

"Indeed. Indeed. We were called 'Quakers' here—because we claimed that we quaked at the Word of the Lord. Many people found that funny, and most people refused to call us by our proper name, the Society of Friends. Friends—that is all we wanted to be." Her voice grew tight, and Josiah thought she might cry. "But everywhere we tried to settle and live our

simple lives, we were pushed away as if we carried some terrible disease. Those of us who stood up for our right to
worship as we pleased were caught like criminals and
whipped—or jailed—or branded like animals. Even Puritans
who talked to Quakers or allowed them into their homes were
punished."

A cold shudder ran through Josiah, and he pulled his
knees up against him.

"Of course, Abraham and Faith Hooker would not be
driven from their faith by anyone. We built our little cabin in
Topsfield and broke ground for planting. Surely if we showed
our neighbors that we, too, were people of God—" She
stopped. "I was still shouting that when they took Abraham
Hooker away."

"Where did they take him?" Josiah said in a small voice.

"I wish I knew, Josiah. I only know he never came back."

"You have lived in this cabin all alone ever since?"

"Not this cabin. They came back the next night and
burned down the house Mr. Hooker and I had built together. I
lived for a while in a hut of skins that Oneko's grandfather
taught me how to make."

"But weren't you afraid? Why did you stay here?"

The Widow Hooker looked at him and smiled sadly.
"Where was I to go? Wherever I went, I knew I would face the
same. At least here, I had my Indian friends."

Questions crowded into Josiah's head like sheep stepping
over each other to get into the pen. He didn't want to know
the answers, but he couldn't seem to keep the questions
tucked away in his mind.

"Why didn't the people of Topsfield come and—take you away, too?"

"At first, I think they assumed I had died in the fire. When someone discovered that I was still here—oh, perhaps years later—the stories of my 'ghost' had grown so—"

"Your ghost!"

"Oh, indeed. I haunted Blind Hole Meadow, so they thought. Many a young lad was snatched away by the spirit of the Widow Hooker, eh?"

She chuckled, then laughed out loud—a crackling laugh that made Josiah want to laugh, too.

"Twenty years went by," she continued. "By then, I had built this cabin with the help of Oneko's family. Those who knew I was still alive were frightened by my friendship with the Indians. Instead of coming to take me away, they protected themselves with stories that gave them an excuse to leave me alone. Ah—and then the Reverend Burroughs came."

Josiah looked up sharply. "The Reverend George Burroughs?"

She nodded.

"He was the preacher in Salem Village when I was born!" Josiah's father had often spoken kindly of the Reverend Burroughs. "He was a man of God," he would say. Josiah's father never wanted to talk about why Reverend Burroughs left the village after only three years, or why the Putnams didn't share the Hutchinsons' love for the minister.

"I was out gatherin' herbs one summer day," the widow said, "and a thunderstorm began to brew. I was on my way back here to stay out of the rain, when I looked up to see a young man with great huge shoulders standing on Misty Hill, gazing up at the sky with the wonder of a small boy." She smiled fondly off into the distance. "The air was sizzling with lightning and the clouds were black and boomin' their thunder like cannons, and still he watched like he'd been charmed. Then all of a sudden he turned, saw me, and said, 'It's a wonder, is it not? Truly, one of God's wonders!'"

The widow kissed the cherry blossom in her hand and blew it back into the air. "And so we stood there and let the rain fall on us and felt the thunder rage around us, and George Burroughs and I became friends. Ah—a man of God he surely was. He was willing to minister to everyone— 'Quakers,' Baptists, Episcopalians—non-Puritans of every kind. Yet, I knew—I *knew*—there were people in Salem Village who would run him off like a raccoon. I knew a good man like George Burroughs wouldn't be welcome here for long."

The Widow Hooker stood up suddenly and shook the cherry blossoms from her skirt.

"King James issued a Declaration three years ago. It said all his subjects everywhere had the freedom to worship as they wished. By law, I am safe now. And still, the hate goes on." She cupped her hand under his chin. "So you see, Big Squirrel, I know all about hate. The only thing I don't know is why it happens—and that was your question, eh?"

Josiah nodded in disappointment.

"I will wager a guess, then." She looked around as if she had a large secret to tell and then whispered to Josiah, "I think people who hate are afraid of what they don't understand." She straightened. "You ask your father, eh? You ask your father, Joseph Hutchinson, if that isn't so. It's a good man, that one."

"But you don't want him to know I know you," Josiah said. "Why?"

The widow sighed. "I've learned a good many things in my time alone up here, and from my friendship with the Indians. Many are frightened by those things. Many are jealous—Dr. Griggs for one."

"Because you know how to birth rabbits and such?"

She laughed her raspy-leaf laugh. "And such. Your father has trouble enough these days without your bringin' more on his head by keepin' company with the likes of me."

"Do you mean I shouldn't come here?" Josiah felt his brows bunch up. He liked the widow even more than he'd known himself.

"That, my Big Squirrel, is for you to decide. But now you must decide to return home."

Josiah looked up at the sky and his heart sank. The sun was already headed for the tops of the trees to the west. "I wish I had Oneko to show me a shorter way."

The widow stared at the line of spruce trees behind him. "You do."

Josiah whirled around, and Oneko stepped easily from among the trees. He grunted softly.

"Does that mean he knows a way?" Josiah asked.

"I think so," said the widow.

Oneko tossed his head, his silky black hair shimmering in the breeze as he trotted off. But he was heading north, away from Salem Village. Josiah took a few halting steps, then stopped.

"Follow him, Big Squirrel," the widow said. "You have much to teach each other."

And so he did. Together they skirted Blind Hole Meadow and traipsed across all of Topsfield. The rows of corn and the pastures dotted with sheep whipped past as Oneko was silently now here, now there, like a wild cat in the woods with Josiah chasing behind.

At the top of Bare Hill they stopped. Below them the Ipswich River raced toward the village. Oneko gave a soft groan. It was the first sound either of them had made since they started their journey. They talked with their eyes, their hands, the tilting of their heads. No words tangled themselves up on Josiah's tongue.

Oneko grunted again and Josiah grunted back. Oneko's face crinkled into a thousand happy lines. Josiah grunted once more and Oneko back at him. Then Oneko gave him a gentle nudge, and Josiah began to run with Oneko in hot pursuit. Josiah spun around a poplar and deftly shinnied up the other side. When he swung onto the first branch, Oneko was already perched on the one above him. With an easy swing, he dropped down and dangled by one arm. He bobbed his head and grunted. Josiah laughed and swung like a possum from his branch by his knees and waggled his head upside down. With a delighted squeal, Oneko let go of his branch, grabbed Josiah on the way down, and toppled to the ground with him.

Arms wrapped around each other, they tumbled down Bare

Hill. Brown skin melted with white. Black shiny hair tangled with sandy curls. Clunky boots bumped against bare toes.

They rolled onto the cushion of grass at the bottom of the hill and bounced apart. Josiah landed on his stomach with his boots half off. Happily, he kicked them into the bushes.

Oneko lay on his back framed by buttercups, and Josiah propped up on his elbow to look at him.

He's so different from me, Josiah thought. His nose and mouth and eyes were small and brown as if they were carefully chiseled out of wood with a sharp, shiny knife. Josiah knew his own face was chunky and rounded, like it was shaped from pudding, Hope always said.

Oneko closed his eyes then, and Josiah watched the sun play across the Indian boy's face. *It looks like he's praying,* Josiah thought.

For a moment, they didn't seem so different. Slowly, Josiah rolled onto his back and closed his eyes. It was a warm feeling like the steam from the Widow Hooker's tea.

Then he felt a pull at his side. He opened his eyes to find Oneko grinning into his face. But with a leap he was gone, swinging Josiah's whistle pouch over his head as he headed for the river.

Josiah squealed and tore after him. Oneko left the bank and split the water cleanly with his body, disappearing beneath its sparkling surface. Josiah skidded to a stop at the water's edge. The last time he'd jumped into the river, he'd nearly drowned.

Oneko bobbed up, hair streaming over his face, and waved the pouch in the air.

Josiah's heart sank. It was fun until now. No trying to be as good. No struggling to prove he was smart. But here it was— the dare to do something he knew he couldn't do. Why did he always end up feeling like a brainless boy?

There was a sudden splash, and Josiah realized it was his own body hitting the water. It rushed over his head, but before he could even flail his arms he was on top again. Oneko's warm wet back was beneath him.

Oneko grabbed Josiah's arms, pulled them around his neck, and began to paddle through the water. Like an otter with his son on his back, his feet kicked out behind and carried them both down the river.

Josiah clung to Oneko and squeezed his eyes shut. But the feeling of floating, the feeling of riding the river, pried them open. Below him, Oneko was strong and sure. Around him, the water was free. His arms relaxed and he perched his chin on top of Oneko's head to watch. He was on the "sea," and he was a sailor aboard his own private ship.

Oneko swam for a long time. He paddled in circles and splashed upriver and floated back down before finally taking Josiah to the bank and rolling him onto shore. Then he ripped from the water, shaking its droplets from his hair like a dog. Josiah scrambled back for his boots and then followed Oneko south toward Salem Village.

As they ran, the air was delicious to breathe, and their cackles and chirps snapped crisply in it. It was free. It was good.

When they rounded the last bend in the river before Log Bridge, Oneko stopped short and his eyes darted cautiously.

Josiah grabbed his arm and pulled him into the brush on the riverbank.

They stood on the edge of Deacon Edward Putnam's land, and Josiah saw what Oneko had heard—the deacon slashing his sickle just above the earth. Josiah knew he'd soon turn his back and work his way up another row of weeds. If they waited, they would have a chance to slip away without being seen.

Josiah watched Edward Putnam, his big face red and sour. He muttered in a tight voice as he worked, and everything about him seemed bunched up and bitter, like a plum left too long in the sun.

I wonder if he was ever a boy like us, running in the sun, Josiah thought.

Somehow, he didn't think so. And for a moment, he felt sorry for Edward Putnam. For all the Putnams.

The deacon finally turned his back and moved away, and Oneko and Josiah padded softly downriver. When Fair Maid's Hill came into view, Oneko stopped. The warm glow left his eyes and the guard came into them. Josiah knew that look now. He was too close to the Village.

Good-bye, his face said.

I'll see you again—soon, Josiah's answered back. He turned to go, but Oneko brushed his arm. Softly, he dropped the leather pouch into Josiah's hand.

Then, with steps that made no sound, he was gone.

✢ ⤐ ✢

Chapter Seven

osiah's father wasn't fooling when he promised to add more to Josiah's workload. He rose before the sun to chop and stack wood and feed and water the animals. He could only say a short hello to Ninny before he was called to breakfast, and then only had time to gobble down his hot corn mush and molasses before his father whisked him off to the fields with him.

Spring came early to Massachusetts that year of 1690, and with his new half interest in the Porter sawmill, Joseph Hutchinson took advantage of it to get ahead with his planting. So Josiah walked along the neat furrows his father had made in the soil with his oxen-drawn plow and dropped the seeds neatly into them. By dinnertime each day, his arms and legs ached, and the back of his neck was crisp and red from the sun.

"You won't starve if you eat that more slowly," his mother

would say as he bent over his trencher and gobbled up his stew.

"Good," his father said one day. "What meat is in it?"

"Squirrel," Hope answered.

Josiah set down his spoon and reached for his mug of milk. Big Squirrel had lost his appetite.

He had little time to rest after dinner before he was back at work again. But whenever his father wasn't beside him, he relaxed a little. Weeding the flax fields gave him an excuse to take off his shoes and walk barefoot among the tender plants. While trimming the mulberry trees into a low hedge, he imagined himself and Oneko in a jousting match with toy tomahawks. As he made birch splinter brooms, he dreamed about what he would do with the six cents each would bring if the money were his to keep.

But he couldn't do anything to make the task of fertilizing the cornfields fun. The ground was soggy from the overflow of the river in the spring thaw. The stench of dead fish rose from his bucket like steam as he plodded down the muddy rows, a rag tied across his nose and mouth to keep him from gagging.

As he passed his mother's herb garden that afternoon, the empty bucket swinging at his side, Hope sat up from her weeding and sniffed the air.

"Ugh." She wrinkled her nose and shuddered. "It's you I smell!"

"Do you want your corn mush and your cornmeal and your popped corn?" Josiah shouted. "Then you've got to have the smell!"

"But I don't have to have you!" Hope said, fingers pinching her nose. "Move along!"

Josiah dropped the bucket noisily to the ground and flopped down beside it. "I need rest. This is a fine spot."

"No!"

"Josiah?" said his mother's quiet voice behind him. "Will there be wood for the supper fire?"

"Aye." Josiah sprung up and winced because of his sore ankles.

"Good, then. Let you be at it."

Josiah put the bucket over his head to close out Hope's husky laugh and limped toward the woodpile. The odor of rotten fish shot up his nostrils like sour bullets. He yanked the bucket off and ran while Hope doubled over with laughter behind him.

Only once could he get away to the Widow Hooker's. It was at the edge of the evening, after an early supper, and he barely had time to help her carry an armload of wood and fetch some spring water before he had to go home. But it was worth the run back through Blind Hole Meadow in the near darkness just to hear her happy chatter and watch her nod as he talked, even when his tongue tripped over the words. Oneko was there as always, and he ran with Josiah as far as the edge of Peter's Meadow. They stopped only once when Oneko shinnied up a tree and grinned down at Josiah. Josiah shook his head. His arms ached from working.

At the end of the third day of his new chores, Josiah could barely lift the last load of wood that would keep the fire going from supper till bedtime. He hauled it wearily into the kitchen in his arms—and tripped on the leg of the spinning wheel as he passed. The oak logs clunked to the floor, and Hope bent

over the sampler she was embroidering to hide her laughter.
Josiah felt a flush worse than his sunburn rise up his neck as
he scurried to pick up the wood.

"Be you lame?" Josiah's father said.

"Nay," Josiah answered.

But his mother and father seemed at once to forget he was
there. They bent their heads together, as if they were in the
middle of a serious conversation when he'd arrived.

"Israel Porter says we've naught to do but rely on good
prayer and good deeds in this business," his father said.

Goody Hutchinson sniffed, and Josiah stole a quick look at
her. Their quiet, obedient mother never disagreed with her
husband.

"I know, Deborah," Papa said. "I know Thomas Putnam
and his brothers and sons flooded that piece of land themselves to blame it on the sawmill. But we have the laugh,
d'y'hear? That land never belonged to them in the first place."

"They resort to foolish pranks—things Josiah or his friends
might think of," his mother said.

It was Hope's turn to give an almost-silent sniff.

"*They* do. Israel says *we* must not—and I am agreed."
Joseph Hutchinson gripped the arms of his chair as Josiah had
seen him do so many times. It meant the next words were the
important ones, the ones that would end the conversation.
Josiah went after the log closest to his chair so he wouldn't
miss them.

"Israel Porter is a Salem Selectman, the only farmer to
have any political power in the town. He is a respected man in
this village, as are all the Porters, and the Proctors—and the

Hutchinsons. The Putnams will not force us to lower ourselves to their mean and dishonest ways. They will not stop us from working our land as we see fit, and—"

This was it. Josiah grew as still as a stone.

"And they will not stop us from taking our places among God's chosen people. On the next Sabbath, we will go, all of us, to Salem Town and return to the church there. I was raised in that parish, and I know we will be welcome there."

Josiah could not keep his face from breaking into a grin. Salem Town! Every Sabbath! He had not smelled the salt air or seen the sea since he was eight years old—

"Josiah! What are you about under there?"

Josiah jumped, banging his head on the underside of the chair. Hope fell into a coughing fit.

"Our son has taken to crawling about like a farm animal," Joseph Hutchinson said to his wife. He shook his head. "Off to bed with you now, both of you."

Hope whipped past him on the winding stairs as Josiah wearily climbed up. He groaned as he lay on his bed. The ropes underneath were growing loose and the mattress sagged under him.

"Stop your complaining," Hope snapped. "Do you think you are the only one who has to work?"

"*You* didn't chop wood until—until your back—mine is nearly ripped in two!" Josiah said.

In the darkness, he watched Hope's white cap pop out from behind the bed curtain. "Why do you suppose you had to chop so much wood, boy?" she said. "Because *I* had to stand over a kettle, over the fire, stirring soap with a stick all day and breathing in fumes of lye that stung my eyes like the fire itself. Eh?" She sat up straighter. "*I* had to cook that stew you gobbled down like a savage at noon. *I* had to add corn-meal a pinch at a time for hours to make *you* a corn pudding with no lumps in it. *I* had to sand the floor to clean it and polish the hearthstone and scrape the trencher that *you* ate from. Eh?"

The words always spit from Hope's mouth like sparks, and Josiah grew tired of getting burned. He tried to gather a few to fire back.

"You hate me, then," he said.

There was a stunned silence, and then Hope threw herself under her covers.

"Good *night,* boy!" she said in disgust.

You must, Josiah thought. *Because you don't understand me.*

No one did. Except for Oneko and the Widow Hooker. They didn't care that even when he meant well, his tries at doing good always crumpled into some huge mess—and that when he tried to explain, the words only added to the stupidness of it all.

They—the widow and Oneko—never tapped their feet impatiently or threw words at him they knew he could never throw back. They knew his thoughts and seemed to know where they came from.

With a sigh, Josiah snuggled into his bed. Hope and her friends had a secret hiding place, but now, so did he. Only he wasn't sure he was ready to show it to William and Ezekiel yet.

Josiah was shoveling spoonfuls of pigeon stew into his mouth the next day at noon when Papa began to grill him.

"Are the animals fed and watered?"

"Aye."

"Has your mother enough wood for the fire to last the day?"

"Aye."

"Are there weeds yet among the vegetable plants?"

Josiah looked at Hope.

"Nay," she said.

"Good then. The sheep must be herded up to Hathorne's Hill and allowed to graze. That is still open land, and John Proctor is sending his boy and Benjamin Porter his to do the same. Both of you go—and mind your hands are not idle while you're about it."

"You can spin on the rock," Mama said to Hope.

Josiah loved to watch his sister make thread for spinning on a hand staff. She was so good at it, she could do it while she walked.

"Josiah?" his father said.

"I shall—I'll find—"

"Be off with you."

"They are good children," he heard his mother say as he tore past the window toward the sheep pen.

His father didn't answer.

From the top of Hathorne's Hill, Josiah could see that spring had, indeed, come to Massachusetts. Below, on his farm and even the Putnams', the fruit trees were alive with fluffy blossoms. Along the banks of the Ipswich the poplar trees were breaking out in delicate green, and everywhere the bare twigs of the maples were tipped with swelling red buds. Josiah stood amid the noisy sheep and looked down at the willows. He grinned. They looked like porcupines with their sharp yellow-green shoots poking out. Soon their branches would be heavy and dragging the ground with leaves, forming shadowy green caves beneath them. The willows made perfect hiding places for spying on sisters.

"Why are you standing there smiling like a ninny at nothing?" Hope said sharply. "The sheep are grazing. Busy your hands."

You are not my mother! Josiah opened his mouth to say. But shouts from below drew them both to the hillside.

"Hope! Hope Hutchinson!"

There was no mistaking Sarah Proctor's happy screech. Josiah pulled his whistle from its pouch and jumped up onto a rock to blow it. An answering whistle tweeted from below.

"William! Up here!" Josiah called.

William's blond hair, so blond it was almost white, blew up in spikes in the crisp air as he tore up the slope. Josiah broke into a run in the other direction, but William's arms wrapped around his legs and they both tumbled to the ground.

"I give!" Josiah shouted. William was a head taller and heavier by several hams' weight. Josiah knew better than to wrestle with him for long.

"Brainless boys," Hope said to Sarah. She nudged Josiah with her toe as he scrambled up. "Sarah and I will watch their flock at the bottom of the hill. Do you think you and William can tend ours up here without getting into mischief?"

Josiah twitched inside his clothes. He hated it when Hope played Mama, especially in front of his friends.

"Aye," he muttered.

"Sisters," William said as he watched their retreating backs. "Good riddance, eh?" He nudged Josiah in the ribs.

Josiah gave Hope one more look. Her job was easy. The Proctor "flock" consisted of six sheep. William's father, John, owned an inn on Ipswich Road that did more to support the family than their farm. But John Proctor wanted his son to know how to work the land, so Sarah and William worked as hard as the Hutchinson children. Sarah, too, complained about Abigail Williams and Betty Parris and their easy life. Josiah couldn't imagine life with the Reverend Parris being easy, no matter how little work you had to do.

"So, are you going to tell me?" William stretched out on the new grass and began to pull the petals off a wild rose.

Josiah flopped down beside him. "Tell you what?"

"About the Indians! You weren't lying, were you, when you said you were carried off by Indians?"

"No!"

William chewed thoughtfully on a rose petal. "Ezekiel said you were."

"He's the liar!"

Josiah saw the twinkle in William's eyes as he sat up. "All right then! Tell me!"

But the sound of another whistle piped from below, and after it, from over the gentle crest of the hill, Ezekiel Porter tramped, eyes huge above the sharp cheekbones that made all the Porters look alike. He carried a gangly lamb that he dumped on the ground between them.

"This is your 'flock'?" William laughed.

"Rachel has the others below," he said. "We've not that many sheep left. My grandfather says we must think more about the sawmill." He poked Josiah, as everyone seemed to be doing today. "We'll be rich, eh?"

"The Indians!" William's straw hair almost stood up on end with the suspense. "Tell us about the Indians!"

Ezekiel dropped next to the lamb, which began to suck on his finger. "Oh," he said. "That lie."

"I don't lie!" Josiah said. "I was not carried off by Indians. I was carried off by *one* Indian. A boy, as old as we are."

"You lie!"

"His name is Oneko."

William and Ezekiel looked at each other, and Josiah bit his lip. He hadn't meant to tell them that. He didn't want to tell them anything. Words would make his friendship with Oneko seem thin and flat. Especially *his* words.

"How do you know that's his name?" Ezekiel said slyly. "Does he speak English?"

"No," Josiah said miserably.

"You made it up then!"

"No! The widow—the widow told me."

Ezekiel's eyes grew larger and his cheekbones seemed to sharpen. "Who is the widow?"

"The Widow Hooker?" William said.

Josiah jumped. "How—how did you know?"

"She haunts Blind Hole Meadow!" William cried. "Her ghost, I mean."

"No!" Josiah's tongue was tight. "No—she's alive—she never haunted anyone!"

"I know," Ezekiel said importantly.

William's admiring eyes turned to him. Ezekiel rolled onto his back and studied the sky. "The Widow Hooker, you say?"

"Aye."

"I've heard her spoken of by Dr. Griggs. He says she's dangerous."

"Dangerous!" Josiah felt the hair on the back of his neck standing up like the spikes on William's head. "I've seen her help birth baby rabbits in a box, right on her hearth—and bring one of them—back to—save its—bring it to life!"

Ezekiel rolled his eyes. "Dr. Griggs says she practices medicine, and she cannot even read. He says her kind of doctoring is dangerous to people."

"Ha," said William Proctor eagerly. "My father says Dr. Griggs knows as much about curin' people as these sheep do."

"Dr. Griggs is afraid of what he doesn't understand," Josiah added.

William and Ezekiel stared at him for a moment, and then Ezekiel threw his head back and laughed.

"You're soundin' pretty high-minded, Josiah Hutchinson," he said. "Where did you learn that?" He wiggled his head mockingly.

Josiah's lips burst open. "The widow tau—she said—"

"You don't know the widow! If you did, they'd put you in the stocks. She's not a Puritan."

"I do know her!"

Ezekiel leaned in, his eyes in slits. "The proof, Josiah."

Josiah looked at him and then at William. Both were waiting, neither believing. The thoughts tore at each other in Josiah's head. The widow wouldn't want him dragging these foolish boys into her life to show her off as if she were some rabbit he'd shot and brought home like a prize. But if he didn't take them to her, they'd never believe him. And it would be the same as always—William strong, Ezekiel smart, and Josiah the brainless boy.

A shriek of laughter below them pierced the stillness of the moment. Ezekiel gave Josiah one last glance and rolled over on his stomach to look down the hill. "Look at them there with their heads all bent together," he said. "That's what we should be doin'. They're plannin' their next escape even now."

William crowded beside Ezekiel, squeezing the lamb between them. He bleated miserably until Ezekiel stuck his finger in his mouth again. Josiah let out a relieved breath and fell beside them. For the moment, they'd forgotten.

Below, surrounded by a handful of chewing sheep, sat Sarah Proctor, Rachel Porter, and Hope Hutchinson on a golden carpet of dandelions. Hope was talking excitedly, hands waving as she spoke, but the boys could hear nothing but an occasional squeak from Sarah.

"She has a voice like a—"

"Like a rabbit having babies," Josiah finished for him.

"I wish we could hear what they're plannin'," Ezekiel said. "They're plannin' somethin', you know."

"Let's get closer." William started to wriggle down the hill, but Josiah put a hand on his leg. Hope would hear even the slightest move. She could hear a ladybug crossing a leaf, he was sure. Josiah nodded toward a stand of pines and spruces just beyond where the girls sat. The spruce were already thick and green and would hide them as they climbed the straight, sturdy pines and cedars for a better spying point. William and Ezekiel read his thoughts and slithered down the back side of the little hill, tossing the bawling lamb among Josiah's sheep as they went. Josiah took a last look at the flock. They were chewing contentedly.

A squirrel scampered down the cedar Josiah chose, and he stopped to let him pass. Josiah imagined that he chittered "Thanks, cousin," as he went by.

Using his knees the way Oneko did, Josiah slithered up the tree ahead of William and Ezekiel. When he reached a high branch, he forgot for a moment why he was there. Below him stretched Salem Village, the only home he had ever known. The houses, their roofs naked now from the blankets of snow, dotted the hills and meadows and farms here and there as if dropped like blueberries onto a corn cake. His father had said many times that part of the little town's troubles occurred because there was no central town common where folks could gather and come together in their thinking. But Josiah loved its sprinkling of houses, even if half of them belonged to the Putnams.

Out of habit his eyes traveled to Sergeant Thomas Putnam's farm, surrounded on all sides by twisted fences that seemed to cry, "Stay out!"

As he stared, movement caught his eye in the pasture where Thomas Putnam's few remaining cows grazed.

Someone was down there. The sergeant's farm was not doing well, Josiah had heard his father say. They had had a run of bad fortune for several years—bad crops, sick and dying cattle. Perhaps even now someone was about to tend to a sick cow. They all looked sickly to Josiah.

The tree creaked slightly as he leaned forward to watch the figure at the fence who didn't seem interested in the cows at all. He was tugging away at the fence rails, as if trying to tear them loose.

For an instant, the figure looked around him. *He wants to make sure no one is watching,* Josiah thought.

In that instant, Josiah caught a glimpse of his face. He looked exactly like Giles Porter.

It can't be, Josiah thought. Giles was Ezekiel Porter's older cousin, about 21 years old and strong as an ox. He was his grandfather Israel Porter's pride, and Ezekiel often talked of wanting to be like him. Why would Giles Porter be tearing down Thomas Putnam's fence?

Israel Porter is a respected man in this town, as are all the Porters, he could hear his father saying. *The Putnams will not force us to lower ourselves to their mean and dishonest ways.*

Then it couldn't be a Porter down there. Josiah strained again to see the figure who had by now pulled a rail from the fence and was carefully resting it back on the posts. Once again the man looked around him, and Josiah gasped. Those certainly looked like the wide Porter eyes and the sharp Porter cheekbones.

Josiah slipped down from the tree without a sound and glanced up at the neighboring pine. Ezekiel was halfway up, his hand cupped around his ear as he strained to listen to the girls. Silently, Josiah crept from the stand of trees and ran toward the Putnam farm. He had to know for sure, and then he could tell his father.

☦ ⚜ ☦

Chapter Eight

By the time Josiah reached the edge of Hathorne's Great Swamp, he was breathing like a bull, and stopped to lean on Thomas Putnam's fence. Panting and puffing, he looked straight down the rails to where the skinny cows picked without interest at the grass.

No one was there. Josiah was sure this was the part of the fence he had seen from the tree, yet it looked as it probably had when the sun came up on it that morning, every rail and post in place.

It was damp and chilly down in this boggy place, and Josiah shivered and looked over the swamp that bordered Thomas Putnam's property. Then he blinked and stared harder. Someone was moving quickly away, toward the river.

Josiah looked over his shoulder and then crept toward the corner of the fence. None of the cows even stirred as he went. Ninny would have bleated a cry for all of Salem Village to hear if someone was on their property who didn't belong there. An uneasy feeling lapped at Josiah's stomach, but he crept on. His father would want to know about this. Maybe at last he could be of some help.

Until he reached the corner of the fence, the rails and posts and the pegs that held them together looked as if no one had touched them. In years, in fact. Josiah's father often joked that the Putnams were so busy running after everyone else's business they didn't have time to take care of their own. But the fence was still standing, until Josiah touched it lightly and the top rail crashed to the ground.

Real fear clawed at Josiah's insides, and he grabbed for the fallen piece of wood. As he did, his elbow hit the lower rail and it too tumbled to the muddy earth.

For the first time, the cows moved, all of them toward the gaping fence.

Grasping with fingers that wouldn't cooperate, Josiah tried to lift the lower railing back to its place before the cows could trample over him and out of their pasture. But the end of the pole hit the corner post, and it leaned crazily for a moment and then plopped into the mud.

"You there! What are you about?" a voice cried out. Josiah looked around wildly—and up into the eyes of Sergeant Thomas Putnam.

"Oh," he said. "So it's you—young Hutchinson."

"Your fence was—it fell—sir," Josiah stammered.

"Aye, a fence will fall if it's ripped apart. Look what you've done!"

Thomas Putnam's hard, colorless eyes scanned the ruined

fence and the cows that trotted heavily past them and off toward the swamp. Josiah's father would have gone after his livestock. Thomas Putnam let them go and turned on Josiah.

"Your father put you up to this mischief, did he not?"

"Nay!"

"Then it was Israel Porter. The Hutchinsons would never do such a thing as this without the Porters had told them to first!"

Josiah shook his head in confusion. All he had to do was tell Thomas Putnam that it was Giles Porter who wrecked his fence, and he would release his painful hold on Josiah's arm. Then Josiah could run back to Hathorne's Hill, back to his sheep and his friends.

But he couldn't tell. Ezekiel wouldn't be able to look him in the face. And what about his father? Wouldn't his father be disappointed in the Porters? Unless, of course, he already knew—

Putnam shook Josiah's arm roughly. "What do you have to say, boy?"

"I—I—don't—"

"Joseph Hutchinson has a boy with pudding for brains. Speak, I say!"

The words stuck in Josiah's throat and he choked on them. "Fix it—I was tryin' to—fix it—"

Thomas Putnam threw his huge dark head back and laughed. "You're wantin' me to believe that a Hutchinson, young or old, would for a moment care about anything belongin' to a Putnam—unless he was claimin' it as his own?"

All the right answers tangled into a ball in Josiah's head.

He tried to pull his arm away, but Thomas Putnam squeezed his fingers tightly and held on.

"We shall pay a visit to your father," he said through his teeth. "And may God have mercy on your soul."

In all the years he had known Thomas Putnam, Josiah had thought things like, *He has a nose like a hill of snow after we've sledded down it.* Or, *He has a fearsome big head, big as a bull's on tiny shoulders!* Now he wondered how he could ever have thought the man silly. As he dragged Josiah, half running, half pawing the air with his feet, across Wolf Pits Meadow to the Hutchinsons' farm, Josiah knew he was nothing but a monster. Fingers dug into his skin, and angry yanks threatened to tear his arm from his shoulder. Josiah couldn't utter a word.

Once he thought he heard voices calling his name, and he searched the hills whipping by for friendly faces. If his friends or his sister did see him, he knew they would flee in terror when they saw who was clutching his arm and hauling him home.

"What are you looking for, boy?" Thomas Putnam said harshly. "More Porters? More Proctors to help you?"

Josiah shook his head and blinked back the tears.

They stopped only once on the long journey. As they passed Reverend Parris's house, the minister stepped out onto the porch of the square, brown parsonage.

"What have we here?" he called to Thomas Putnam.

"Hutchinson's boy. I found him tearin' down the fence on my northwest pasture."

Josiah missed the minister's answer. He watched as a face

pressed itself against the narrow glass in the front of the house. Abigail's eyes looked closer together than ever as she stared out at him. *No wonder Hope wishes you would go back to Barbados,* Josiah thought. Even the smile that curved the corners of her mouth was mean. Josiah couldn't pull his arm from the iron grasp, but he stared back at her until she looked away.

"It is surely vengeance for his not bein' elected a church member," Reverend Parris said above Josiah's head.

"Aye," Thomas Putnam answered, and with a cruel jerk on Josiah's arm, he was off again.

They were only a few minutes from Josiah's house now. What should he tell his father? That he'd seen Giles Porter working his mischief? That he'd seen him from a tree while spying on his sister, instead of tending to the sheep?

Josiah squeezed his eyes shut. The sheep. The flock was probably scattered from here to Topsfield by now. First the stray calf, now the sheep. Would the day ever come when he *didn't* bring shame on his father?

Joseph Hutchinson was waiting at the gate as they rounded the last curve. With one final pinching squeeze Thomas Putnam shoved Josiah's arm loose, and he fell against his father's chest.

"Stand up, boy!" his father said. The flames of fear crackled in Josiah's heart.

"I've brought your boy home, Hutchinson!" Thomas Putnam said.

"So I see."

"I found him on my property."

"Did you now?"

"Tearing apart my fence!"

There was a silence. Josiah stole a glance up at his father. Papa's bushy eyebrows had shot up like two question marks.

"Tearin' up your fence, you say?"

"Indeed. He was tryin' to put it back together when I found him."

"'Tis a curious thing, don't you think, Mr. Putnam, that the boy would tear down your fence only to put it back together before you found him?"

Putnam's face turned the color of a beet, and for the moment the fear stopped lapping at Josiah's insides.

"Was he havin' any luck at it?" Josiah's father said.

Thomas Putnam gave a hard laugh. "He could barely lift the rail—"

He stopped, and Joseph Hutchinson nodded slowly. "Easy to see, then, how the boy could rip the rails from their very pegs and off the posts—" He looked right into Thomas Putnam's eyes. "When he couldn't even lift one to put it back together."

"You're always twistin' people's words—"

"Go back to your farm, Putnam. It was your own people who tore down your fence to let your scrawny cattle free so you could blame it on one of us. Get off my land, Mister."

There was a silent stare-down, and through it Josiah had a flicker of hope. Maybe his father was right. Maybe the figure he'd seen from the tree *was* a Putnam.

But as quickly as the thought passed through his mind it clouded over. That was no Putnam with a big head and funny-shaped nose. It was a Porter—handsome and strong, and with eyes big enough to see when it was time to run away.

Josiah stared sadly at the ground, and then his father roughly lifted up his chin to face him. Out of the corner of his eye he watched Thomas Putnam stomping off in the dust.

"I'll go—" Josiah stuttered. "The sheep—I'll fetch them — I'll fetch them home!"

"Ach! Your sister has already brought them home, along with the news that Thomas Putnam was standin' in front of Samuel Parris's house with you danglin' from his hand like a rag doll." He shoved back Josiah's sleeve and inspected his arm. Bands of red encircled his flesh.

"What were you about, sneakin' around Putnam's pasture?" he asked.

Josiah opened his mouth, but no words came out. He searched the ground but found none there, either.

"Josiah! Answer me!"

"I thought I saw—someone—tearing apart the fence. When I got there—he was gone. I only touched the fence— and it—fell."

"Who was that someone? Did you see who it was?"

Giles Porter, Papa! That's who it was. The grandson of the man you look up to as your own father. They do lower themselves, Papa! Do you?

But none of those thoughts crossed his lips, and Josiah stared back at the ground. Finally his father tapped his shoulder.

"Ach—you couldn't see a face from Hathorne's Hill, I'll warrant. Go to your mother."

But I'm not a baby, Papa! Josiah wanted to scream. *Don't send me to the kitchen to do baby chores! I was tryin' to help you.*

"She'll see to your arm," Papa said. "And tonight see that you do your sister's chores after supper, as well as your own, since she brought the sheep home alone."

There were no "but's", no "That is not fair's!" You didn't shout those things after Joseph Hutchinson. But the words fought to get out of Josiah's throat as he watched his father walk away. And even as he gazed, Goodman Hutchinson whipped his head back over his shoulder.

"Out of my sight, boy! If I didn't know better, I'd say the good Lord didn't give you a brain to think with!"

Then he turned and was gone, leaving only his words, stinging Josiah all the way to his heart.

✢ ✢ ✢

Chapter Nine

Josiah was able to slip away on Saturday afternoon for a visit to the Widow Hooker. Her blue eyes danced when he told her they were going to Salem Town for the Sabbath.

"You like the sea, do you, Josiah?" she said.

"Aye. I want to be a sailor someday."

She cocked her birdlike head to one side. "Not a farmer like your father?"

Josiah scowled and she laughed her sprightly laugh.

"There is no need for words from you, Big Squirrel. Your face talks for you. Can it tell me then why your father is taking you all the way to Salem Town to worship?"

"My mother and father weren't elected members of the church in Salem Village," he explained. "My father won't go where—he thinks—where he doesn't belong."

The widow nodded wisely. "Your father and I are of the

same mind. It's a good man, that one."

The widow spent time in her herb garden that day, and when Josiah followed her out to watch, he heard a thin, high-pitched whistle from the edge of the trees.

"What was that?" he asked. "What bird?"

The Widow Hooker chuckled. "The Oneko bird."

Josiah crept cautiously toward the stand of spruces and listened. He heard it again—and caught a glimpse of brown skin between the branches.

Josiah dug into his leather pouch and pulled out the latest wooden whistle he'd carved. Softly at first, he blew.

A slow wail answered from the woods.

Josiah wormed his way closer and blew again. The whistler blew back.

As Josiah raised his whistle to his lips, the branches split and Oneko was on him. Squealing and clawing, they rolled to the edge of the herb garden.

"Wild Indians, both of you." The widow's whole face twinkled.

Show me your whistle, Josiah's face said.

Oneko held out two fingers. Between them was a blade of broad grass.

Josiah's eyebrows formed a question mark.

Oneko pinched the grass neatly between his two thumbs and put them up to his mouth. When he blew into the grass, it gave out a thin, piercing wail.

Josiah grinned.

Oneko pushed it toward him. Josiah took it, pinched it clumsily between his thumbs and blew. But he got only a handful of spit. Oneko showed him again, and after at least ten tries, Josiah got a squeak. Oneko's face crinkled, and then he held out his hand. Josiah pulled the wooden whistle out of his pouch.

"You keep it," he said.

It rained all the way home, and Josiah went to the barn with Ninny to dry off before he slipped into the house and upstairs. He was afraid it would rain all night, and that the family wouldn't make the journey to Salem Town for Meeting.

But the sky was pink and rosy as Josiah came out of the barn the next morning with Ninny in tow. His father was walking up from the road, kicking the mud from his boots. Josiah knew he was inspecting the wagon to make sure it would make it through the thick puddinglike mud caused by the rain.

"See that your sister is up and about," he said to Josiah. "We must make an early start."

By seven o'clock, the Hutchinsons were tucked into the wagon, drawn by two of their four oxen. Hope and Mama sat low in the back, wrapped in their capes to keep the dust off of their plain homespun cloth dresses. They wore no ribbons or bows, for anything fancy was scorned as vanity among the Puritans. But Hope's bright eyes and crimson cheeks couldn't be dulled. Josiah knew she was as excited as he was.

But Josiah sat high on the front bench with his father. He loved to listen to him mutter and bark at the oxen. It was almost like a song. And the sight of his father's strong arms bulging under his cinnamon-colored broadcloth coat as he skillfully drove the animals made Josiah sit straight and try to puff out his own shoulders under his woolen jacket.

"What are you *doing,* boy?" Hope said.

But Mama clicked her tongue at her and Hope was quiet.

They were only a farm away from their house when Papa drew the reins in and the wagon lurched to a halt.

"What's this now?" he murmured.

"Hutchinson! Whoa, there! I say, whoa, there!"

Deacon Edward Putnam stepped boldly into the road and stood in front of the wagon. The oxen dipped their heads within inches of the foxtail pole he waved.

"Brainless man," Joseph Hutchinson muttered under his breath.

"And where might you be goin' this Sabbath morning, Goodman Hutchinson?" Putnam asked.

"I don't see what business that is of yours, Putnam," Papa answered. "I have a right to drive Salem Village streets as I please."

"That you have." Edward Putnam stepped to the side of the cart and looked up at the Hutchinsons. He had the smallest shoulders of any of the Putnam brothers. To Josiah, that made his large head look even bigger.

"But," the deacon went on, "I am the tithing man. You know that. It is my office to make sure you'll be back to Salem Village before the morning Meeting, or you know you will be charged a fine for not goin' to church."

"And why is that?" Joseph Hutchinson said. "If you will remember, Mr. Putnam, I am not a member of the church at Salem Village. You and your brothers have seen to that."

The deacon's big head began to redden. "The Lord has

seen to that, Hutchinson! If your covenant with God were pure—"

"Begone with you!" Joseph Hutchinson's voice was deadly quiet. "I've a mind to go to the church in Salem Town, and that's where I'll go. Now get out of my way or I—and these oxen—will run you over. Good day."

Deacon Putnam didn't move. Papa picked up the reins, slapped them sharply and the oxen jolted forward.

"Joseph!" Mama cried.

But Josiah's father shouted to the oxen, and before the deacon could dive for his life, the wagon was on its way. With a terrified screech, Edward Putnam fell backwards into the mud.

"Joseph! You've hit him!" Mama cried.

"Good," Papa answered. And with another slap at the reins he drove the oxen down the road.

"You'll pay for this, Hutchinson!" Edward Putnam shouted after them. "And don't think you'll get out of payin' your dues to Reverend Parris and this church—"

His voice was drowned out by the clopping of the oxen's hooves, and Mama's praying in the back of the wagon.

Josiah was doing a little praying himself. *Lord, let the stocks not be waitin' for Papa when we get back.* The picture in his mind of Willard and Cheever dragging his father to the pillory in front of the Meeting House didn't look good at all.

As they drove through town, cold stares and turned backs met them at every corner. Nathaniel Ingersoll stood in front of his inn with his arms folded, his eyes daring Joseph Hutchinson to try and come in. Nathaniel Putnam, Edward and Thomas's brother, let loose of the pig he was carrying and let it run between the oxen's legs to stop the wagon. But Joseph Hutchinson didn't stop. The pig squealed and Nathaniel Putnam turned red and shouted.

All the while, Josiah's father, his broad shoulders squared, kept his eyes on the road ahead of him. Once Josiah heard him mutter something. He thought it was, *Lord, help me.*

It grew quiet in the wagon, and soon they reached Ipswich Road, the well-traveled path leading them to Salem Town. In spite of the uneasiness that chewed at Josiah's stomach, he sat up straighter on the seat and looked around. Except for flights on foot to Proctor's Inn to fetch William now and then, he seldom had the chance to go down Ipswich Road, and he wasn't going to waste this one. From the sound of Edward Putnam's threats, this might be his last chance for a while.

The Ipswich Road formed the dividing line between Salem Town and Salem Village. They were once one town. But the two places were very different from each other, Josiah had heard folks say. The farm people lived by their land and worked with the weather and seasons to make their way. The people in Salem Town lived on the sea harbor that was formed by a spider web of rivers; they were ruled by the tides. Most were merchants who worked at sending cod and mackerel, furs and horses, grains and meat to the other colonies and to faraway places with names that made Josiah dream. Names like the West Indies and the Canary Islands.

Their lives were different and so were their ways of thinking. The people in Salem Village wanted their own church and the right to make their own rules and take care of themselves, and Josiah's father agreed. Even though Salem Town still had control of the village, he was happy when they built their church and called their own minister.

But Josiah also knew that his father was against the bad feelings that had built up between the villagers and the townspeople. Many a night he'd heard him arguing with the Putnam brothers and Nathaniel Ingersoll by the Hutchinsons' fire.

"Why do you think the farms were made here in the village?" he would hear his father say to them.

"Because the people of Salem Town drove out the God-fearing farmers!" a Putnam would say.

"Nay! Because the soil there wasn't rich enough to supply them. Their Selectmen made grants of land—to my father, and yours, Putnam and Ingersoll—and Porter, too. Without the farmers in Salem Village, the merchants in the town have nothing to ship. And without the ship owners in Salem Town, we farmers have nowhere to sell our goods."

"I grow crops to feed my family!" Thomas Putnam would cry. "I am not of a mind to sell them."

"Then soon you won't be able to feed your family at all," Josiah's father said one night. "Because the times are changin'. Along with Boston, Salem Town is one of only two main points of entry to Massachusetts. Half of what is imported to or exported from this colony is passed right through there. We cannot blink at it—we must be a part of it."

That was the last night a Putnam came into their house.

No matter what the problems were, the ride along Ipswich Road enchanted Josiah. It crossed three rivers that flowed into the Salem Harbor. They all had wharves and landing places from which goods could move by water between village and town, so trades of all kinds peppered the side of the road. Josiah looked for the signs hanging over their doors. The potter had his shop there, and the carpenter and a shoemaker.

There were taverns and inns, too, like Proctor's Inn, which was a mile south of the Salem Village line. William always repeated stories he'd heard from the travelers who came from places as far away as Boston. Josiah knew the Ipswich Road went all the way to Boston, but it was a place he only dreamed of going to.

"The roads are good," Josiah's father said at last to break the uncomfortable silence. "God willing, we'll get no more rain before we return home."

The wagon lurched over a rut and Papa turned his attention to the oxen.

Any more mud, and we'd have been stuck in that one, Josiah thought. But even that sounded exciting. Anything was better than hauling wood at home.

As soon as they drew near to Salem Town, Josiah smelled the sea air. It was a mixture of fish and salt and was like no smell you could sniff in Salem Village. It sent excitement sizzling through Josiah.

His father turned the wagon down a narrow Salem Town road blocks from the harbor, and the oxen suddenly seemed clumsy and odd amid the finer wagons that lined the street. Josiah glanced back at Hope. She was crouched low in her seat, as if she were ashamed to be seen. But her dark eyes came just to the top of the wagon and darted about.

The trumpet signaling the start of the Meeting was already sounding when they slipped into the dim church. A tall, stately man, with elegant hair to his shoulders and a beech walking stick with ivory and brass trim, met them at the door and grasped Joseph Hutchinson's arm warmly. He whispered into his ear and pointed to a bench. Mama and Hope slipped into it, next to a woman whose snowy white collar was tipped with lace. Lace and silk collars were outlawed in Salem Village, and Josiah saw Hope gaze at it—so hard that she tripped on the bench and landed headlong in the woman's lap. Josiah put his hand in front of his mouth.

He felt a sharp poke at his shoulder.

"Josiah Hutchinson! There will be no mockery in this church, d'y'hear?" His father's breath was hot in his ear.

"Aye," Josiah said meekly.

"Let you sit on the steps, then, and be about your prayers. And for once, try and stay out of mischief."

The gallery was already full of boys, so Josiah took the place his father nudged him to, halfway up the side steps that led to the loft. He would feel uneasy among the town boys anyway, especially without William and Ezekiel. The Porters planned to stay at the village church for a while, Ezekiel had told him. And Sarah Proctor had told Hope that her family wasn't going to church at all, which was against the law in Salem. Josiah thought of John and William and Sarah and their mother Elizabeth all in the stocks—perhaps next to his own father. He shivered.

The Meeting began, and Josiah looked curiously over the railing. Up the aisle came the Reverend John Higginson whose name he had heard often in his house growing up. His father respected the reverend the way he did old Israel Porter. *Maybe you aren't worth respecting until you are at least 70,* Josiah thought as he watched the bent and white-haired minister make his way to the front of the church; you didn't spit pumpkin seeds at a man with a wise face like Reverend Higginson's.

The plump man who sat at the front of the church with Reverend Higginson was a different matter. Rolls of flesh bulged from his collar, and his bright red cheeks were so round, they pushed his eyes into tiny poke holes. If William and Ezekiel were here, they would all find a way to get this man's flabby chins jiggling with fury.

It's better that they're not here, Josiah thought. *I must not bring shame on my father today.*

One look at his father, and Josiah was sure of that. On the seat next to the tall man, Joseph Hutchinson sat proudly, his broad shoulders relaxed. There was no circle of hate around him but only peace for him here.

The psalm and the opening prayer ended, and everyone settled in for the sermon. Josiah watched the sand trickle through the hourglass and got his hands ready to cover his ears. It only took Reverend Parris about a quarter of an hour to work up to the shouting.

But the Reverend Higginson's voice stayed soft. He talked about God's love as something they would see and understand when their lives were over and they met their Lord. But for now, he explained, it was a special gift they could almost hold in their hands.

When Meeting ended, Josiah was careful not to run from the steps, which meant he was nearly trampled by the pack of boys who ripped down from the gallery like squirrels. He found himself carried out to the churchyard as on the crest of a wave.

The sudden glare of the sun blinded him. Blinking against it, Josiah stuck his hands in front of him to grope his way. One hand punched into the middle of someone's back.

"Ach!" A tall young man with red hair that stood in spikes whirled around, his eyes flashing. "Who struck me?"

Five arms shot out and pointed at Josiah.

"He!" they shouted.

Josiah shook his head until his brain seemed to slosh against the insides of his skull, but the red-haired boy moved toward him, one fist punching the palm of his other hand.

"I beg your—I couldn't see—the sun!"

"Josiah!"

Josiah turned toward his father's voice. The red-haired boy took that moment to grab him by the shirt front. He held him out, straight-armed, and Josiah smacked the air wildly with his fists.

"What is the meaning of this?" said another voice, a thick voice.

The boys scattered, leaving Josiah and his attacker in full view of the churchyard. Josiah's arms went limp, and the red-haired boy let him fall to the ground.

"The young scamp was tryin' to rip me, Reverend Noyes," he said. "I was hard put to hold him off me."

The other boys murmured their agreement, and the puffy-faced minister glared down at Josiah.

"Reverend Noyes!" came a shout. "That be the Hutchinson boy. Fetch him here!"

From a corner of the Meeting House yard, Reverend Higginson called to them. Josiah's parents and Hope were with him.

"Come then." With pinching fingers, the Reverend Noyes took hold of Josiah's ear.

If I do meet God when my life is over, Josiah thought as he was dragged across the churchyard, *I'm going to ask Him why He allowed men who hate children to become ministers.*

Behind him the boys hooted among themselves, and his face burned.

"My assistant, Mr. Nicholas Noyes," Reverend Higginson said when they reached him. "Joseph Hutchinson and his good wife Deborah. These are their children—"

Mr. Noyes sliced the air with one impatient hand while he continued to pinch Josiah's ear with the other. "You're from Salem Village, Mr. Hutchinson?"

"Aye."

"Why are you not at Samuel Parris's meeting this morning?"

The whole churchyard seemed to wait for his answer.

Joseph Hutchinson looked straight into Nicholas Noyes's tiny eyes. "I had a notion I'd feel more of God's presence in this church."

"And did you?" Mr. Noyes demanded.

Josiah's father didn't falter. "In Mr. Higginson, sir, I believe I did."

Reverend Noyes waggled Josiah furiously. "If you intend to make a habit of worshiping with us here," he said, cheeks jiggling angrily, "may I propose that you leave this young criminal at home? He's not here two hours and already he has stirred up trouble among the boys."

"Shall we go to my house, Joseph?" The tall man who had greeted them at the door appeared out of nowhere and put his hand on Papa's arm. Everyone was still. "There is a noonday meal waiting there for you and your family. Please, come be our guests."

"Now, then," said the lady with the lace-tipped collar who had also melted into the group unnoticed. She took Hope's arm. "You very nearly sat in my lap, and we've not even been properly introduced! My name is Mary English, my dear." She looped her other arm through Mama's, and the three walked off chatting.

Reverend Noyes puffed out his cheeks, gave Josiah a final shove, and stalked off. Reverend Higginson bowed politely and moved to another group of townspeople. Josiah rubbed his ear and tried to look invisible.

"Pay Nicholas Noyes no mind," the tall man said quietly to Papa when the ministers had moved away. "He has the ideas of a stubborn old man, and he's barely thirty. It's Higginson who runs the church, and he thinks as we do."

"Thank you, Phillip," his father said.

Phillip English looked down at Josiah. "Reverend Noyes has no patience with the injustices that come to young boys, that's sure. How is that ear, son? Shall we send for the doctor?"

Josiah's father laughed, a sound Josiah hadn't heard in a long time, a sound that jolted him to attention. "If my son

Josiah were taken to a doctor every time some angry Puritan dragged him home by some part of his body, I'd have to sell three of my fields just to pay for it!"

"He's a scoundrel, is he?" Phillip English ruffled Josiah's sandy curls. "You must spend some time at my house, then. I've two baby girls. A little boyish horseplay might bring those rooms to life."

Almost as if by some unseen hand the anger was scattered, and the three of them walked easily down the hill toward the harbor. Josiah shook with relief.

"It's a good boy, Joseph," he heard Phillip English say.

The English house was a mansion on Essex Street, and Josiah was certain the minute he walked in that this was not a house where boyish horseplay would be welcome. In the front hall, rich banisters made of dark, shiny wood curved along the stairs—up to heaven, Josiah decided.

"Come, we'll dine upstairs." Mary English led the way to the second floor.

They ate at a long, smooth table—the wood was called teak, Phillip English told them—under a painting of Mary English with two round babies. The servants, she explained, had whisked them off for their naps. Josiah caught Hope's look. The subject of servants always lit up her eyes.

But the sight that brought the light into Josiah's face came when the heavy curtains were drawn back to let in the afternoon sun, and he looked out the window. There in all its dazzling sparkle was the harbor, dotted with the 21 ships of Phillip English. While Hope gazed at the French linens on the table and sipped the West Indian coffee, Josiah could not take his eyes off the vessels that brought those things—from France and Spain and Portugal and England. The conversation went on like a dream behind him as he drank it in—the grand ships, the waves splashing against the docks, the sailors rushing about with their thick, heavy ropes. Only when Phillip English's voice rose to an excited pitch did Josiah turn from the window.

"Of course you will be accepted here! Your father was a member here, Joseph. You came to this church as a young boy—and we know you to be a godly man, one of God's chosen, surely."

"My ideas are different from my father's," Goodman Hutchinson said.

"These men are not farmers, Joseph. They have seen the world and their minds have broadened. Look you—Mary and I were Episcopalians when we came to Salem. Products of the Church of England herself. We wanted to build an Anglican Church here! But we soon applied for permission to join the First Church in Salem. We made our covenant; we were accepted. You will be, too."

"I trust that the Reverend Higginson knows my sort. But Noyes—"

"Nicholas Noyes!" Mary English said.

All the Hutchinsons looked at her in surprise. Deborah Hutchinson would never join into a conversation like this one. It was unusual for her or any Puritan woman even to remain in the same room when men were discussing serious matters.

"Let your mind rest easy," Mrs. English said. "You come to Salem Church, and you'll be welcomed."

"God knows you're a good man, Joseph," Phillip said quietly. "And we know it, too."

The adults continued to talk, and Josiah went back and forth between listening and watching everything around him. Outside, the ships bobbed in the harbor and Josiah imagined himself aboard one, squinting into the sun as he mapped out his voyage.

Inside, words flew. Words about getting lumber from village to town. About the ships it would sail on. About the prices it would bring. Only his mother didn't speak. She looked out of place sitting on the edge of the velvet-cushioned chair in her severe Sunday black. Josiah watched her put her china cup on the table and clasp her red, gnarled hands in her lap as though to hide them. His eyes followed hers to the delicate white fingers of Mary English, which gaily caught the air as she talked.

Not so Hope. Her cheeks were on fire with the wonder of it all. *She's imagining herself mistress of this house,* Josiah thought. *And wouldn't she be beautiful in it?*

Josiah shook his curly head and stared out the window. She would never think such kind thoughts about *him.*

The spring rain fell, hard and steady, as they came out of the afternoon Meeting, and the streets were already oozing with thick mud. Josiah and his father pulled their wide-brimmed hats down over their ears, and Hope and her mother took shelter under a blanket in the back of the wagon.

"Perhaps we should not have stayed for afternoon Meeting," Goody Hutchinson said.

"Perhaps not," said Papa. "But my soul has thirsted for words such as those I heard today." He clucked almost cheerfully at the oxen. "We'll be home soon enough. God provides."

They were barely out of Salem Town before the wagon's wheels were covered in inches of mud. The oxen's hooves pulled heavily at it, making a sucking sound as they trod.

"This rain will be good for the crops!" his father shouted over the torrent of raindrops. "And the higher the river, the better the sawmill runs. There will be enough for the Hutchinsons—and some to spare for Phillip English to sell in the colonies."

Josiah peered in surprise from under his dripping hat. The rain was hitting his father's teeth, he was smiling so broadly.

"See you hold on now!" his father said. The wagon pitched roughly to the left, and Josiah clung to his seat to keep from being thrown into the mud. As the wheels met the ground again, the wagon lurched in the other direction and Josiah landed against his father's shoulder. "We're in for heavy seas!" Papa said.

The rain continued and the miles stretched longer. For a while Josiah pretended the rocking of the wagon was a wave tossing their ship—a ship like the one that had enchanted him from the window. But a sudden slide into a slushy rut jerked him back to the wagon. The going was so slow that darkness set in before they were even close to Salem Village. Even Proctor's Inn was over a mile away.

Goodman Hutchinson pulled the oxen to a halt and stared at the black road ahead. Then he studied Josiah.

"Do you think you can do one thing, Josiah—and do it just as I tell you?"

Josiah nodded.

"There's a lantern in the back of the wagon. Walk ahead of us a few steps with it—high above your head. You can light our way and perhaps keep us out of some of those ruts we have before us. Can you do that?"

His mouth asked the question, but his eyes already held doubt in them.

He quickly lit the tin lantern and put it into Josiah's hands. Then, plodding heavily through the mud, Josiah got himself in front of the wagon and stuck his arm straight up in the air. Anyone from Salem Village who saw it would know them by the lantern. Each family had its own pattern of holes which they poked in the tin. The light shone through and proclaimed "Hutchinson!" or "Porter!" The Putnams' pattern, he remembered, was a crown. "That's how highly they think of themselves," his father always said.

Josiah swung the lantern and marched through the mud. No matter what his father thought, he would lead his family safely home. No matter what—

With a slow-motion slide, Josiah and his Sabbath Meeting clothes were backside down in the muck.

He scrambled up to keep from being trampled by the oxen, lifted his knees, and broke out farther in front of the wagon. Rain poured in torrents off the brim of his hat and mud oozed into the tops of his boots, but he pushed into the darkness.

"A *huge* rut!" he cried out. The wheel would be buried if the wagon went into it.

"You must guide me around!" his father yelled back. "I'll move to the right of it!"

Josiah stood on the slightly higher ground between the deep gullies in the road and swung the lantern to guide his father. Papa slowed the oxen to a crawl until the front left wheel was even with the rut.

Josiah swung the lantern. "Too close!" he cried.

"I have no choice. There is a deep ditch on the other side!"

Josiah held his breath as the front wheels bordered the rut and slid crazily as they passed it. Mud caved in, but the front part of the wagon passed freely.

"Now we've the back to do!" his father shouted. "Call out loud now!"

Josiah kept his eyes boring at the rut as the wagon bounced forward. He waved frantically to the right.

"I've no more room!" his father shouted.

The back wheel teetered at the edge of the hole and Josiah prayed hard. Slowly, his father eased the wagon forward, and the wheel began to slip.

"No!" Josiah wildly swung the lantern over his head while his father snapped the reins and shouted at the oxen. The wagon careened and swung as the animals strained through the mud. With a violent, sickening slide the wagon took a final lurch, and the wheel hit the bottom of the rut.

Screams rose from the back of the wagon. Josiah looked up in time to see his sister fly though the air.

✝ ⚜ ✝

Chapter Ten

osiah didn't know whether to laugh or cry.

The wagon hopelessly mired in the slime and was something to cry about.

Hope sprawled, face down, in the same mud—Josiah could barely keep from snorting out loud.

"Hope!" his mother cried from the back of the wagon. "Are you hurt?"

Hope only screamed. It was the kind of scream she let out when Josiah put a frog down her back. He was sure she wasn't hurt.

"Fetch her, Josiah!" Goody Hutchinson said. "Be quick now!"

Still swinging the lantern, Josiah mucked his way through the rain to where she lay, spread-eagle, in the mire. He leaned over and grabbed her arm.

A black face glared at him. "Don't touch me!" Hope cried.

"I'm helping you up!"

"Nay! I am perfectly able to—" Hope grunted, plunked her hands firmly on the mud, and at once sank to her elbows.

"Let me—"

"Nay! Don't touch me!"

"What are you about down there!" Josiah's father shouted. "Is she hurt?"

Josiah reached down to grab her arm again and felt sharp teeth sink into his skin.

"Ow!" He jumped back and landed squarely on his backside beside her.

"What in the name of heaven?" Papa's voice boomed. The big hands grabbed Josiah under the armpits and yanked him up. "Are you hurt?" he asked Hope.

"Nay," she said miserably.

With one hand Papa pulled her to her feet. She crossed her arms over her chest and began to shiver.

"Fetch her a blanket," Papa barked.

"*I* shall fetch it myself." Hope staggered toward the wagon, teeth chattering.

It *was* growing colder and the rain felt icy as it slid down Josiah's back. He followed his father's eyes to the stuck wagon. Perhaps now it was time to cry.

"Can the oxen pull it out?" his mother said.

"Nay. We need the strength of at least one more animal. Even a horse would do it." He studied the sunken wheel for a long moment, then looked wearily at Josiah. "Take the lantern and see if you can find a branch or small log. Perhaps we can create a lever."

"She's freezing," he heard his mother say as he took off to the woods. "We must get her home or she'll be sick sure."

Josiah quickly found two fallen oak branches and dragged them back to the wagon to his father. His father jumped with one of them into the rut. The sides came up to the tops of his legs. He carefully placed the log at the edge of the wheel and pushed the mud until the branch was securely under it. Its end stuck out near Josiah's face.

"Shall I take hold of this end?" Josiah asked.

"Nay! I'll do it alone."

Josiah knew if he helped the lever would work better. Gingerly, he put his fingers on it.

"No, Josiah! In your clumsiness—if the wagon turns over I'll be crushed, and you with me. Stand back now!"

His heart sinking nearly to his boots, Josiah stepped back and watched as his father put his hands around the log close to the wheel. His veins bulging, he pushed on the branch. The wheel rose only a few inches, and the wagon rocked uneasily.

"That should work, then," he said.

No, it won't, Josiah wanted to scream. *It would work better if I helped. I can do it!*

"Deborah—you drive the oxen now, when I say. I'll push here and we'll have her out."

Without a word, Deborah Hutchinson gathered up her skirts and climbed into the front of the wagon.

"Get you back," Papa said to Hope and Josiah.

Hope moved to the high side of the road, dragging her blanket with her. Josiah stayed as close as he dared, his back toward his sister. He couldn't take her mocking eyes now.

"Have you the reins?" Joseph called to his wife.

"Aye."

"Wait!" Hope cried. "A horse!"

They all stopped to listen, but it was several seconds before the rest heard the clopping of hooves from afar.

"Josiah! Take the lantern and hail him! Quick now!"

Josiah grabbed the lantern and tore to the high spot where Hope stood.

"Whoa, there!" Papa shouted, and Josiah held the lantern over his head. From out of the darkness, the horse emerged up Ipswich Road headed toward Salem Village. The horse slowed for a moment and the rider, too, held up a lantern. Josiah leaned out with his.

"Whoa, there!" Joseph Hutchinson shouted again.

But the rider kicked out his heels and before they could see his face, the horse flew past them and off into the darkness. He came so close, the wagon rocked in his wake.

"Whoa! Whoa, there, I say!" Papa shouted after him.

"Who was it?" said Mama.

"I could not see his face."

Josiah hadn't caught his face either, but only one family in Salem Village could ride like that. And he'd seen something else besides. The rider's lantern had the pattern of a crown.

"Putnam," Hope muttered beside him.

With Goody Hutchinson driving and Papa working the log, it took nearly an hour to push and pull the wagon out of the mud. Josiah's arms ached to grab the log and help. When the wagon finally came free, his father called out, "To the front with the lantern!" Josiah bolted onto the road before Papa could change his mind.

For a mile, Joseph Hutchinson drove the wagon, with Josiah scouting ahead for more danger, and Hope and her mother walking behind. Josiah could guess what was going through everyone's minds. Were there wolves about? Bears? Robbers?

Putnams?

Josiah didn't add Indians to his list. He hoped, in fact, that Oneko would fall from a tree and together they could guide his family home by some magical path. Teamed with Oneko, he could do anything.

All four were wet and weary when they reached Proctor's Inn. Even after they were given dry clothes and some of Goody Proctor's lentil soup, Hope and Josiah were too tired to share the day's excitement with Sarah and William. Josiah did see Hope whisper to Sarah as Sarah took her bowl to be washed.

"They're planning something, sure," William hissed to Josiah. "We must be watching these next few days."

Josiah's father spoke in low tones to Goodman Proctor. "Some villager passed us on horseback and stopped not even for a minute to see if we needed help."

"Putnam, d'y'think?"

Joseph Hutchinson nodded soberly. "Aye. I could tell by the way he sat in the saddle. I'm sure of it."

Josiah could barely get out of bed the next morning. His arms ached, his legs burned—and Hope's coughing had kept him awake most of the night. He poked her as he went past with his boots in his hand. She groaned under her quilt.

"Brainless boy," she started to say. But the words were lost in a fit of coughing. She sounded as if she had stones in her chest.

As Josiah gathered the eggs and dreamed of ships and the sea, his father called him into the barn. "I've business to attend to," he said. Hard lines showed in his face today. "I must go to the sawmill and then to Israel Porter. It's time you learned that business, as well."

"The sawmill?" Josiah said.

"Take the small hand wagon and go to the river. Israel Porter's grandson Ezekiel will meet you there. You two gather some stones, this size." He shaped his hands. "We can use them to repair the walls at the mill."

Josiah's heart sank. He'd hoped for a moment that he would be allowed to go to the mill and see what his father was about there. But only for a moment.

Josiah took the eggs into the kitchen, where Hope sat at the table, toying with her corn mush with a wooden spoon.

"Eat," her mother said.

"I am not hungered," she said, lower lip pouting.

"Are you sick, then?" Josiah asked.

Hope made a face. Mama clicked her tongue at both of them. "It's berries you're wantin' on that mush," she said. "Take the basket and fetch some. The woods must be full of them, if the squirrels haven't taken them all."

Hope's pale face lit up, and Josiah knew her thoughts.

The game is on, brainless brother, they said.

Hope was out of the house like a bolt of lightning, but Josiah dragged his feet as he went for the hand wagon. He was sure to hit a Putnam in the head with a wagon full of river rocks or something equally stupid if he went off after Hope. Everything he did lately seemed to lead to trouble with his father.

Aye, this was the perfect chance to slip away and see the widow and maybe even Oneko—but that would mean taking Ezekiel. Josiah could prove once and for all that he did know her, and an Indian boy. But it was *his* place—where Hope's teasing and his friends' daring didn't matter.

"Will you be off, then?" his father shouted at him.

Josiah grabbed the hand wagon. First the rocks. Then maybe the right answer would come to him.

The wagon rattling behind him, Josiah took the back path to the woods that bordered the Porters' place. With the house in sight, he called out. Ezekiel shot from the barn.

"Papa says you're to help me load this wagon with stones," Josiah said.

"That'll be done in no time." Ezekiel's big eyes slanted. "Let you take me to this widow's cabin after, eh?"

Josiah began to stammer, and Ezekiel pulled his mouth into an ugly bunch. "You're nothing but a braggart, Josiah Hutchinson," he said. "You never knew no doctorin' widow, nor no Indian, either." His voice went to a hiss. "You're a lyin' sinner."

All the thoughts that tugged at each other in Josiah's mind suddenly fell apart, and Josiah could see nothing but the sneer on Ezekiel's face. Just like the one on Hope's face. And his father's.

"Come on, then," Josiah said through gritted teeth. "I'll take you there."

They crossed Goff's Bridge and stayed hidden in the brush and trees along the tiny Porter River where they piled stones into the wagon and hid it in the tall grass. Then they cut to the woods that lined the road to Topsfield. From time to time, Josiah looked back for Hope, but she was nowhere in sight.

The air was deliciously crisp after the rains, and the Widow Hooker's door was thrown wide open to let it into the cabin.

"Hallo!" Josiah called, poking his head in.

"Where is she?" Ezekiel said.

"Not here. But she can't have gone far. The fire's still burnin'."

"Hmm." Ezekiel looked around suspiciously. "Where's her Indian friend?"

"He doesn't *live* here," Josiah said. "He just visits."

Ezekiel shot up an eyebrow and looked into the box on the hearth. "I don't see any baby rabbits, Josiah Hutchinson. But of course, with her powers, they're probably already full grown and having babies of their own by now, eh?"

He laughed, and the hair on the back of Josiah's neck stood up.

"Are you callin' me a liar, Ezekiel Porter?"

"Nay. I'm sayin' you may be seein' strange things in the dark—when you're asleep!"

"You'd better take that back," Josiah cried.

"And *you'd* better get out of here," a voice spoke, "before I tell Papa you've been consortin' with strange people."

Josiah whirled around. Hope stood in the doorway.
"What are *you* doin' here?" Josiah said. His heart was
suddenly slamming against the inside of his chest.

"I might ask you the same question." Hope stepped into
the cabin and touched the petals of the tiny buttercups gathered in a bowl on the table. "This doesn't look like a Puritan
home, Josiah. Should you be here?"

"Should you?" Josiah sputtered.

"I followed you. I must look after my little brother"—she
stopped and coughed harshly—"when he's too stupid to look
after himself." She covered her mouth to smother another
cough and held up her finger. "I hear something!"

Ezekiel grabbed the edge of the table, eyes wild. Josiah
looked out the window. The Widow Hooker was several
hundred yards away with her back to them, filling her basket
and looking peacefully over the field.

Anger bubbled up inside Josiah. The decision was made—
he didn't want Ezekiel or Hope to know the widow. They
could call him a liar until he was old and shriveled. He wasn't
giving up the one friend who didn't think he was a brainless
boy.

With a shove, Josiah pushed Ezekiel toward the door.
"Don't let her catch us in her house!" he hissed. "We can hide
in the trees until we are sure it's clear and then we can make
a run for it."

Hope gathered up her skirts and skittered out in front of
them. They all landed in a heap just inside the stand of spruce
trees. Hope pulled her apron in front of her mouth to
smother the coughing and laughing. Ezekiel looked around

madly for an escape route. Josiah glared at his sister.

"Have you—are you finished—did you pick all your berries?" he hissed.

"Have you finished *your* work?"

"Aye!"

"Good, then. Because you will be doin' most of mine for a while."

"Why?"

"Because that is the only way you will keep me from telling Papa what I saw up here today. You payin' a visit to a suspicious person—someone obviously not a Puritan, eh?"

Josiah closed his mouth and looked at her darkly.

"You may choose," Hope went on. "But I would not want to be in your boots when he finds out that in order to keep you safe, I, as your older sister, had to follow you all the way to Topsfield—"

"What would you have me do?" Josiah said wearily.

"You may start by gathering the rest of the berries." She smiled sweetly as she handed him her basket. "Then, of course—"

The list went on all the way back to Salem Village. By the time they parted so that Josiah could pick up the wagon of stones, he had another day's worth of chores added to his own. Hope sat down to catch her breath, and Josiah decided she looked too pale and sickly to do them anyway.

✝ ⋯✝⋯ ✝

Chapter Eleven

I fear it will rain forever," Hope moaned. A cough rattled her chest, and she shoved her sampler angrily into her lap.

Josiah agreed, but he would never admit it. He wasn't speaking to her anyway.

For five days he had done most of her chores as well as his own, without letting anyone know he was on double duty. The worst part was enduring it while Hope laughed behind her spinning wheel or over the string of candles she was making. Those were the only jobs he couldn't do for her without someone noticing. She'd laugh silently when he came in with a basket of eggs in one hand and a load of wood on the other shoulder, after having fed her chickens and pulled the weeds from her vegetable garden.

Then she would go into a fit of coughing so bad she'd have to stop and catch her breath.

"Josiah, clean these dishes for your sister," his mother told him on Saturday after supper. "She needs to lie down and rest. That cough is becoming worse."

Even as she curled up in front of the fire on the settle, Hope's eyes were sparkling.

But they weren't sparkling now and neither were Josiah's. It had rained for three days and it was still pouring. There were no chases through the woods, no escapes to pick berries. No trip to Salem Town for church—and no visits to the widow.

It was nearly dark now, on the Sabbath, and they had sat in the house all day. Joseph Hutchinson had read to them from the Bible that morning, and they had prayed together and spent the afternoon with their own thoughts. By the time supper was cleared, Josiah felt like a Quaker.

The iron knocker on the front door clanged noisily, and Joseph Hutchinson looked up from the book he was reading by the fire. Even through the smoke from the rush lamp, Josiah saw that the lines were deep in his face.

Goody Hutchinson went into the hall. Her face was pale when she led their company into the kitchen. Behind her were Reverend Parris and Deacons Putnam and Ingersoll. Thomas Putnam brought up the rear.

"Good evening," Joseph Hutchinson said stiffly.

The men nodded to them all and waited to be asked to sit down. Josiah's father said nothing.

Reverend Parris pointed to the book in Papa's hand. "That be not the Bible, Mr. Hutchinson."

"Nay," Papa said.

There was another uneasy silence.

"Hope," said their mother nervously, "see to those apple tarts in the cupboard for our guests. I shall lay a fire in the best room—"

"There will be no need for that." Goodman Hutchinson looked at his wife. She nodded her understanding and held out her arms to the children.

"Upstairs," she said quietly.

Josiah flopped miserably on his bed, but Hope went directly to the window and opened it. The misty rain danced to get in, yet Hope settled herself on the windowsill and leaned out.

Josiah's mouth fell open. "What—"

"Hush!" She waved him off as if he were an annoying fly and tilted her ears to the open window. She was listening hard, and Josiah knew if anyone could hear what was happening below, it was she.

Whatever it was, it was sure she wouldn't be sharing it with him. Josiah lay flat on his bed and drifted off to sleep.

It seemed only a few minutes had passed when he was jolted awake by the sounds of angry voices. He didn't need Hope's keen hearing to know what they were saying.

"You have a duty to give your share of the money that pays my salary!" Reverend Parris's voice boomed through the floorboards.

"Nay!" came his father's angry tone. "Not to the minister of a church where I am not allowed to belong!"

"You'll be jailed if you don't pay!" Thomas Putnam roared.

"We'll see to that, Ingersoll and I!" Josiah knew that was Edward Putnam. He was sure his big head was purple by now.

"Worse than that, Mr. Hutchinson," said Reverend Parris, "you cannot count on the salvation of your soul if you refuse to worship as a Christian."

There was a heavy silence. Josiah imagined his father's eyes piercing them all from under his fierce eyebrows.

"How?" he said finally. "How can any of you call yourselves Christians when you live as you do? Blaming others for your own misfortune. Refusing to stop and help your neighbors when they're in trouble. Excluding people from the church out of jealousy."

Thomas Putnam gave a hard laugh. "Why would any of us be jealous of you, Hutchinson? You, who have turned on this village—"

"Turned on it?"

"Aye! You're a traitor. Everyone in Salem Village knows you've taken up with Porter's sawmill to become involved in trade with Phillip English!"

"Aye!" his brother chimed in.

Now Papa was the one to laugh. "And is there some new law that the good people of Salem Village Parish Committee have conjured up which says I may not?"

"No!" cried Reverend Parris. "Every man may use God's blessing as he pleases—as long as he is not greedy, Mr. Hutchinson—as long as my salary is paid first!"

"You men are ugly and twisted with your jealousy!" Josiah could hear the edge of laughter still in his father's voice. "I don't know that I want to be a member of the First Church of

Salem Village. It seems all of its members are so afraid of new ideas, of anyone slightly different in thinking from themselves, they've forgotten why our fathers and grandfathers came here. It was for the love of God—but I hardly ever hear that mentioned in your church anymore, Reverend Parris."

Josiah heard muttering and shuffling below, and then the door slammed. The men's angry voices tangled together as they passed under the window. Hope closed it quietly and went to her bed.

Josiah rolled over but his eyes wouldn't close. Behind him, Hope sniffed and coughed—and sniffed again. Josiah sat up and peered at her through the dark. The shadows of her shoulders on the wall were shaking. Taking a deep breath he said timidly, "Are you crying?"

"Everything used to be so clean and clear!" she burst out. "Black and white—like a white collar on a black cloak! There was morning—and there was night! There was winter—and there was summer!" She pulled her hands through her black curls. "Now everything is as gray and—and—mushy as that mud out there! And I'm stuck in it!"

Josiah understood what she meant. It used to be that there was Porter, and there was Putnam. There were the Puritans—and there were the godless. Now it was all confused.

Hope was sobbing hard. Josiah clutched awkwardly at his quilt.

"I'm frightened," she said. "And that makes me angry because I don't like to be frightened—and when I'm angry I'm always mean and snappish."

"I know," Josiah said.

He half expected her to throw her bedclothes at him, but instead she padded across the floor and sat on the edge of his bed. The tears ran down her cheeks.

"Please, Josiah, there is a place I must go to tomorrow. It's the only place where I can make things seem right in my own mind." She grabbed hold of his hand for a brief second. "I promise I will never ask you to do my chores for me again—but for one day, will you please, if Mama or Papa ask where I am—will you tell them I've—gone to—" Her hands flailed helplessly.

"To gather kindling in the woods," Josiah said. "We're running low."

Surprise flashed in her dark eyes.

"Good, then," was all she said.

When her coughing finally stopped and her rattled breathing became even in the bed across the room, Josiah lay awake for a long time. *Where could she go that would make everything clean and crisp in her mind again? I would like to go to that place myself.*

They didn't have to lie to Papa about the kindling after all. Right after breakfast the next day, they were sent to weed the onion field, a full day's job on the other side of the farm.

"Perhaps a day in the sun will do that cough good," Mama said to Hope. "I've tried every cure that comes out of my herb garden. If it doesn't go away soon, I'll have to ask Dr. Griggs."

Hope made a face, and Josiah couldn't blame her. Most of Dr. Griggs' medicines were pretty foul tasting.

They had pulled weeds for about an hour when Hope stood up and listened.

"Papa's gone on his horse," she said.

"Sawmill," Josiah said. "Go now."

Hope's face grew soft as she looked at him. Josiah ducked his head.

"Thank you," she whispered. And she was gone.

For a few minutes, Josiah continued to weed, working double time to get Hope's share done before she returned.

But thoughts began to pop into his head—like unwanted bugs into a sack of flour.

A place where I can be clear and crisp in my mind again. I would like to find a place like that.

If it were you, Josiah—don't you think she'd follow you?

Didn't she follow you to your secret place—and spoil it for you?

Josiah shoved a handful of weeds into the basket and looked around. He could just see her disappearing into the trees behind the Meeting House at the bottom of Thorndike Hill. Even as he watched, she stumbled, caught herself and staggered on. He hoped wherever she was going it wasn't far. She wouldn't make it.

Quickly, he got up and began to run. Wherever she was going, he was going, too.

It was hard to stay far enough behind her to keep her from knowing he was there and still follow. She fell several times and once had to stop to catch her breath from coughing. Josiah watched as she leaned against a tree at the base of Solomon's Hill, her face almost as gray as its bark. The sunlight hit her cheeks, and he saw tears.

Maybe I should leave her alone and turn back, he thought guiltily.

But when she mounted Solomon's Hill and began to cross Blind Hole Meadow, Josiah's guilt faded. A strange feeling took shape in the pit of his stomach. She couldn't be going— where it appeared she was going.

The Widow Hooker's cabin was quiet in the clearing as Hope crossed to it—until Josiah heard his elfin friend's voice greet his sister in the doorway.

"God's own Hope!" she cried. "Ah, we have tears today, eh? Come in—"

In the stand of spruce trees, the thoughts tumbled through Josiah's brain in angry confusion. *The widow is my friend. I found her—and this place. How dare Hope—?*

Then new, even angrier thoughts poured in. *She has been coming here all along, but she used my friendship with the widow to get me to do her chores for her!*

Josiah's fists doubled against the final thought he didn't want to think. *The widow knew that Hope was my sister. Why didn't she tell me? Why did she let me go on acting like a foolish boy who had discovered something secret and special?*

That one last furious thought brought him out of the trees. He would march into that cabin and tell them both—

But before he could take three steps he was on the ground, with a warm, wiggling body on his back.

✛ ✛ ✛

Chapter Twelve

His attacker rolled him three times on the ground, and though Josiah kicked and pulled, he couldn't get loose. Blindly, wildly, he bared his teeth and bit. He found himself on his back, staring into a brown face.

"Oneko!"

The Indian boy grunted and nodded.

"What—I have to go! Those women—the widow and my sister—they've made a fool of me!"

In answer, Oneko straddled him and sat on his belly.

"Oneko! Stop—what—"

Stubbornly, Oneko shook his head and folded his arms.

"Let me—go!"

Brown hands pressed down on his shoulders.

"She's been sportin' with me, Oneko!"

Oneko's face came up suddenly and he looked sharply toward the cabin. When he rose onto his knees, Josiah rolled onto his stomach and stared through the tree trunks.

Hope had appeared in the cabin's doorway. The Widow Hooker put a hand softly on his sister's forehead, and she smiled. Oneko crept to the edge of the trees to watch. Josiah crawled after him, but Oneko looked at him with eyes that said, *Do not disturb this moment.*

It did look like an important moment to Josiah, and he watched in wonder as the widow pulled off her shawl and pressed it into Hope's hands. They looked at each other like two people who understand each other very well, and then Hope walked quickly away. Oneko shot Josiah a warning look.

"I'm going to talk to the widow," Josiah whispered.

But Oneko caught his arm and nodded toward Hope. She passed them in a hurry, but two steps away she coughed and stumbled and caught herself.

"She's ill," Josiah hissed.

It didn't seem so important now—his anger at Hope. She was slipping and coughing and clinging to trees as she gasped for air. The rattling in her chest seemed to fill the woods. Silently, Oneko followed her, Josiah right behind.

They had almost reached Wolf Pit Meadows when Hope's pace slowed nearly to a crawl.

"Don't—don't come into the village," Josiah murmured. "Trouble—there will be trouble for you."

But just then Hope fell headlong into a patch of grass, and Oneko stood still to watch. This time, she didn't get up.

Oneko ran to her like a frightened deer and scooped her up into his strong brown arms.

She'll be screamin' when she sees he's an Indian! Josiah

thought, and he ran to them, to clap his hand over her mouth if he needed to.

But as Oneko loped along toward the Hutchinson farm, her head dangled from his arm, and her eyes were closed. Josiah's insides began to churn. The face that hung there in the sun—was blue.

When they reached the onion field, Oneko laid Hope gently down on the ground. He grunted softly and pointed toward the house. It wasn't until he was gone, vanished without a sound, that Josiah realized he had placed Hope in the exact spot in which she'd stood before she left.

But there was no time to think of that. Heart pounding, Josiah bent over his sister. "Hope!" he cried into her ear. She didn't move but breathed her rattled breathing. He scooped his arms under her, but he couldn't budge her.

"I'll fetch Mama!" And he choked back the tears as he tore toward the house.

The afternoon passed in a blur. When Josiah looked at the events in his memory that night, it seemed that they had happened, surely. But then it was if someone had taken a swipe at them and smeared them all together. Only a few of the details remained.

Josiah and his mother half carrying, half dragging Hope toward the house. Papa, the long lines cracking his face. Hope looking waxy and small on the cot that now huddled up to the fire. Josiah outside the house, Dr. Griggs inside, his face framed in the window, his head shaking.

Josiah had shaken his head, too, but for a different reason.

"No," he longed to tell them all, "we will not shake our heads over Hope. It's my fault—she will be well again. She has to be!"

"She will be," a quiet voice had said behind him.

Josiah looked up to see his father standing beside him. He wiped furiously at the tears rushing down his face in tiny rivers. He hadn't known he was talking out loud.

"We must look to good prayer, Josiah," Joseph Hutchinson said. "Pray. I've a notion your prayers will do much good."

Josiah held that memory still now as he sat huddled on Hope's empty bed in the dark. The silence in their room was lonely, and the thought of that moment with his father kept him company.

Papa had looked down at him for a long time, it had seemed. It wasn't a look that would send him off to feed the chickens or fetch a ladder. It wasn't a look that would scold him for chasing off instead of being at his work.

It was a look like one worried person gives to another when their worries are the same. But Josiah hadn't looked back at his father. How could he pray for God to make Hope well when it was his fault she was sick? If his father could have depended on him, Josiah could have helped with the wagon. She wouldn't have landed in the mud—she wouldn't have gotten a chill and that cough. And if he hadn't covered for her so she could go to the widow's—if they hadn't always sneaked around and lied to go to Topsfield.

Josiah clutched Hope's eiderdown quilt around him now and shivered. When he was ashamed, God seemed so far away. It was so dark, and they needed His light, and Josiah couldn't ask for it. There was nothing left to do—except listen to the hard, rattled breathing of Hope on her sickbed below.

The days stayed dark for the Hutchinsons.

Hope lay on her cot in front of the fire, coughing and wheezing and tossing. Josiah heard her crying out at night, jabbering things no one could understand.

Mama was at her side every minute, spooning drops of chicken broth into her mouth, wiping the sweat from her forehead, tightening the quilts around her, and reheating the warming pan whenever Hope shivered in the steaming room. When Hope slept, Mama set about brewing medicines from the simples Dr. Griggs had prescribed from her herb garden.

"Give her a brew of snake root for the fever," he had said. "Enough to put on a pen knife's point. And rue to help her breathing. Just the size of a walnut."

It didn't seem to do any good. Nor did any of the other cures Mama tried from her medicine book. Her own mother had started the book and she had kept it up, writing down which simples and worts had cured their ills through the years. Mama grew them all in her herb garden. She picked them now, went into the small room that was attached to the kitchen, and ground them into powders with a mortar and pestle and stirred them into broths.

But still Hope tossed and coughed. Once when Josiah's mother dozed in exhaustion in her chair, Josiah crouched next to his sister and stared into her face. All the red had drained from her cheeks, and her fingers twitched on the quilt. Josiah sucked in a breath. She looked just like a fallen leaf, withering, as if before his eyes she might crack and blow away.

It's your fault, a voice in Josiah's head taunted him. *If she dies, it's your fault. You're a brainless boy.*

From then on Josiah stayed out of the kitchen as much as he could. He couldn't stand to hear every breath that sounded like it would tear a hole in Hope's chest. And he couldn't stand the thought that after every breath, he might not hear another one.

There was the work of three people to do, and Josiah tried to do it all. Mama began to look gray, and once or twice Josiah thought he saw her stop and work for her next breath. If she had to worry about weeding the gardens and sweeping the floors, he feared she would surely drop right there in the kitchen and not get up.

Josiah was up well before sunrise every day—feeding and watering, chopping and weeding. The sun usually rose while he was milking the cow, but he never noticed. All the days seemed dark, no matter what time it was. Through it all, there were no games to make the work easier. He didn't dream of leaving the farm and sailing off across the seas with Phillip English or of sitting in the best room with the men and drinking cider. He just worked—hard and alone.

One morning as he milked the cow, he felt a wet nudge at his elbow. When he looked up, warm brown eyes gazed sadly into his.

"Ninny!" Josiah said. "Growin' like a weed, eh?"

He scratched her nose absently and went back to his milking. Patiently, she nudged him again.

"I haven't time now," he told her. "I've work to do. There's hard sickness in our house, did you know it? Hard sickness."

"Ble-e-eh."

Or did she say, *I know. I'm sa-a-a-ad for you?*

"It's Hope," he said. "You remember young Hope Hutchinson?"

Ninny nodded.

"She's not doing well. We're all afeard—. Papa says my prayers may do some good. But I can't pray. I've been—I've been too bad to Hope to deserve much from God."

He sat back on the stool and stared into the bucket of milk. Ninny licked his face with her thick, warm tongue. Josiah realized then that tears were trickling down his cheeks. Patiently, Ninny was licking them off. He put his arms around her neck and sobbed.

"Josiah!"

It was his father. Josiah snatched up the bucket and smeared his sleeve across his eyes as he dashed to the barn door.

"I've the milk right here—" he cried.

His father pushed the bucket aside. "Run—fetch Dr. Griggs! Hope's—run, son—fast as you can!"

Josiah's head hammered as he dug his toes into the dirt and flew across the farmyard. Dr. Griggs lived a good mile away, east on Ipswich Road, almost to Leach's Hill, and Josiah went straight for it. His boots clung to the heavy mire in the marsh, mud slinging from them, as he crossed Nathaniel Putnam's property and hit the Ipswich Road. Nathaniel screeched at him from his field, but Josiah pushed on, clomping across Goff's

Bridge over the Porter River. He'd crossed that very bridge—
so long ago now—with Ezekiel Porter.

He arrived at Dr. Griggs' with only enough breath to tell
him that Hope—Hope needed him—now. Dr. Griggs galloped
off on his horse toward the Hutchinsons' without a word, and
Josiah began the long trudge home.

No use in running back to the farm. There was nothing he
could do to help Hope. And what if he got there—and Dr.
Griggs had not been able to help her, either? As long as
Josiah wasn't there, he wouldn't have to know that for sure.
He slowed his pace to a crawl and plodded past Nathaniel
Putnam's.

"Where are you going with your head to the ground, *boy?*"

Josiah didn't have to look up to know it was Reverend
Parris's niece. There was no mistaking the mocking in Abigail
Williams' voice.

"Well?" she said impatiently.

Slowly, Josiah looked up at her. She stood, arms folded
across her chest as if she were some constable who had a
right to question him.

"Has the devil gotten your tongue, boy?" She looked ready
to stomp her foot in the mud if he didn't answer.

"I was—I tried to—I've been to fetch Dr. Griggs," Josiah
said.

"Why?"

Josiah's neck hairs bristled. "Hard sickness in our house.
My sister Hope."

"I've heard of her illness." Abigail sniffed as if the air were
suddenly full of some very bad odor. "It isn't any wonder, is it?"

Josiah stiffened.

"I've heard them talking—my uncle and the others." She looked around and leaned toward him secretively. "They say your family refuses to come to church—*and* your father will not pay his taxes for the church. Those are *sins* against *God.*"

She widened her eyes and stared hard at him. Josiah bit at his lip.

"Well?" she said. "Have you nothing to say for yourself?"

"No," Josiah said stubbornly.

A mean smile pushed up the corners of Abigail's tight little mouth. "Your sister is dying because God is punishing the Hutchinsons for their sins."

"She is not! She is not—dying!" Josiah flew at Abigail, arms stretched out like swords. The heels of his hands hit her shoulders and shoved her soundly to the ground. A scream rose from out of the dust.

"*You* are in trouble, Mister!" Abigail cried as she pulled herself up from the ground. "You are in trouble with the church! You are in trouble with God! Now you will be in trouble with my uncle!"

Josiah stood rooted to the spot and watched Abigail flounce toward Nathaniel Putnam's.

"Mark it!" she screeched over her shoulder. "God will surely punish you now!"

✚ ✚ ✚

Chapter Thirteen

osiah ran the rest of the way home, away from Abigail's snapping words and accusing eyes. Every footfall beat out the rhythm. *God's punishment. God's punishment.*

When he reached the Hutchinson farm, the beat stopped. Josiah clung, panting, to a poplar.

Joseph Hutchinson stood at the front door with his fists clenched. Ezekiel's father, Benjamin Porter, stood between him and Dr. Griggs who waved his arms about him in self-defense. Their words came to Josiah like scattered fragments of glass.

"I've done all I can—"

"She's not improved a lick since the first day you looked at her—"

"Look to yourself, Hutchinson. Look to God's purpose in this—"

"You'd best send for the Reverend Parris now!"

"Off! Off with you, I say!"

Dr. Griggs retreated down the path, clutching his hat. Josiah's father stalked off toward the field with Benjamin Porter behind him.

Slowly, Josiah walked toward the house. When he turned the corner, he heard the door from the kitchen bang open.

"Deborah! Where are you going?"

Josiah's mother burst from the house, a wooden spoon in her hand. Prudence Porter, Ezekiel's mother, followed her, calling to her.

But Deborah Hutchinson didn't stop. She hurled open the tiny gate to her herb garden and flung herself into the dirt. She was crying, out loud, like a wounded animal, and she dug wildly at the dirt, flinging plants and roots over her head in a rage.

"Deborah! Deborah! What are you doing?" cried Goody Porter.

"What good are these? They can do nothing for my daughter! She's dying! They can die, too!"

She stabbed the spoon into the earth, and Goody Porter threw her arms around Deborah's shoulders and held her. Goody Hutchinson's screams faded to sobs, and they swayed together in the garden.

Josiah fled to the fields, not knowing where he was going, or why. Tears blinded him, and he tripped on a stone, falling headlong into the onion field.

As he rolled over on his back puffs of dust rose toward him, and a large pink nose nuzzled his neck.

"Go away, Ninny," Josiah moaned.

But the calf's brown eyes rolled in fright. Josiah sat up. "What's the matter?" he whispered. "What is it?"

Then, from beyond the fence, came a sound like none he'd ever heard before. Hard, raspy gasps, each ending in a whine of sheer pain.

His father was crying.

"Get hold of yourself, man," he heard Benjamin Porter say.

Josiah ducked behind Ninny and held his hand over her mouth.

"Come. We'll go to my father. We'll go to Israel Porter, Joseph. It's a good man. He will know what you should do."

The two men muttered for a moment, and then Josiah saw them rise from behind the fence and head slowly for the road. He watched, as in the distance, his mother and Goody Porter moved like unreal shadows into the house. The silence hung in the air. Josiah had never felt so completely alone.

Hope was dying, that was sure now. Dr. Griggs could do nothing. The herb garden was of no use. His father had given up. Maybe Abigail was right. Maybe God *was* punishing them.

"No!" Josiah cried to Ninny. She stepped back timidly. "No! God, please! There has to be someone. There has to be someone to help us!"

"Ble-e-eh."

Josiah sank back to the ground, and as he did his hand came down on something soft. It was the Widow Hooker's shawl, the one Hope had worn home that day.

"It must have fallen off as we carried her to the house!" Josiah said to Ninny.

The shawl was damp and dirty now, but Josiah squeezed it tight in his hand. The widow could do things no doctor could do. He'd seen her with his own eyes.

Josiah held the shawl to his chest, and a plan without words took shape in his mind.

The Hutchinson kitchen was quiet when Josiah came in, except for the patter of the evening rain on the windows and the soft talking of the women at the table. Josiah's father was still gone and Benjamin Porter with him. Hope breathed hard, but her body was eerily still. Mama slept fitfully on the settle while Elizabeth Proctor and Prudence Porter stirred soup and talked in hushed tones.

"Have you had your supper, Josiah?" Goody Porter said.

"I'm not hungered."

"A boy not hungry!" The laughter in her voice was forced. "My Ezekiel would never turn down food!"

"I must go and—"

"And what?" Elizabeth Proctor said. "You've done your father proud, workin' so hard. Why don't you rest now? What's so important?"

"Wood!" Josiah cried.

"Wood! There's plenty. The whole house is an oven as it is!"

"I must gather more!" And he fled from the kitchen. Outside, he stood on tiptoe to peek in at his sister, struggling for her life by the fire.

I'll bring her back, Hope, he promised silently. *God willing, I'll bring her back.*

The rain made the sky a dreary gray, but it stayed light until Josiah reached the widow's cabin. He searched through the water dripping heavily from the spruces for the light in her windows. His heart sank. There was none.

His feet sloshed on the soggy yard as he ran to the door and pounded on it. He didn't dare to hope, though. The windows were dark and no smoke curled from the chimney.

But a voice like the crackling of leaves said, "Who is there?"

Josiah almost beat down the door. "Josiah Hutchinson! Please, you must help me!"

The door opened and the widow peered at him out of the dark room.

"Come in, come in! You're drenched, Big Squirrel."

She took off her apron and tried to wrap it around his shoulders. Impatiently, he shook it off.

"I've no fire, Josiah. I can't warm you."

"No—you—must come—to the village—to my house!"

The widow quickly lit a candle and held it close to his face. "What is it, Big Squirrel? There is real trouble, eh?"

"Aye. It's Hope—"

"Hope?" The widow's eyes flickered with fear.

"She's dyin'. Dr. Griggs can't do no more for her—there's no medicine to help her—"

"Dyin'?" She set the candle on the table.

"Will you come with me?" Josiah begged. "You can help her."

"I am not welcome in Salem Village. I may bring trouble on your father."

"He already has trouble—you can't hurt him more."

The widow shook her head. "I'll send you with herbs. You listen close now, and I'll tell you how to use them—"

"No!" Josiah put his hands to his head and pulled clumps of sopping hair. "I cannot! I cannot! I can milk the cows and I can bring the wood and I can kill the chickens for dinner but—I cannot save my sister. I cannot!"

Slowly, the widow nodded. "Of course you cannot. You've followed God's will as far as He's takin' you. He brought you here. Now my work begins."

As if jolted by lightning, she began to bark out orders that sent Josiah scurrying to every corner of the cabin and yard, bringing clumps of this and bags of that. In minutes a basket of simples and worts was packed, and like a bird about to take flight, the widow looked around the cabin.

"I haven't a shawl," she muttered. "It appears to be lost." She stopped short at the door and looked seriously at Josiah. "I'm going to try and make it, Big Squirrel. I've been a bit weak these last days. Too weak even to gather my firewood. Only God's strength will carry us there. We must pray."

Josiah looked at her sharply. In the Puritan faith, it was against the law for a woman to pray out loud, in public. But in the dark, quiet room, the widow put her hand on Josiah's shoulder and began to speak. For a minute Josiah thought she was talking to some other person in the room. Her words were simple and plain, and they calmed the fear that raced through his veins.

"Father, what we are about tonight we cannot do alone. With one of Your great hands, hold Your daughter Hope.

With the other, guide our footsteps to Salem Village. Amen."

Josiah looked up. A light shone through the window.

"What's that?" the widow said.

"God!" Josiah said.

A smile crinkled the cobwebs of her elfin face. "God's messenger, at least."

She threw open the door, and Oneko's face flickered orange in the light of the torch he carried.

"Salem Village?" she said.

He didn't answer. He scooped the widow onto his back and led the way into the woods.

✢ ✢ ✢

ou make a fine horse, Oneko!" the widow cried out. Josiah strained to see her through the rain. He could only keep them in sight if he stayed less than two paces behind. Even though the Indian boy carried the Widow Hooker on his back like a papoose, keeping up with him wasn't easy. Because the marshes were swampier than ever in the rain, Oneko kept to the rocks and high spots, prancing over them like a deer. He never turned to be sure Josiah was on his heels, for which Josiah was grateful. He would hate for Oneko to see him stumbling and slipping his way along like a wet puppy. All that kept him from flopping down under a tree and quitting was the thought of Hope in front of the fire. He hoped God was still hanging onto her.

Oneko stopped only once—when they reached the top of the hill overlooking Nathaniel Putnam's house. Through the downpour they could see the fuzzy light through his window, and across Ipswich Road, the candles flickered weakly in Israel Porter's. A tongue of anxiety licked at Josiah. If his father were to come out of that house right now, what would he say about the Indian who stood beside his son?

Josiah looked at Oneko. His sharp brown eyes were alive with fear.

I can take whatever punishment Papa gives me, Josiah thought. *But can he?*

He turned to Oneko and held out his arms to take the widow. Oneko looked at the lights below for a long moment, then shook his head.

"How much farther is it?" asked the widow. "Perhaps I can walk."

In answer, Oneko pulled her legs tighter around his waist and sprang down the hill. Terrified, Josiah ran after him.

"No!" he shouted. "Not that way!"

But it was no use. There was no other way to go except to wade through the swamps that were quickly filling up with rain. That would mean dipping the widow in cold water up to her waist.

Josiah's head whipped from one side to the other as he scanned the road, but so far it seemed empty. Ahead of him, Oneko stayed close to the trees. Josiah stopped and looked around carefully. The best route might be to loop down around the south woods. It might take longer, but it would be safer.

"Oneko!" Josiah hissed into the dripping darkness.

There wasn't a sound.

Josiah called louder. "Oneko!"

"Whoa, there!"

Josiah froze. Heading toward him down the street was a lantern. It bore the pattern of a crown.

Thoughts screeching in his head like a thousand birthing rabbits, Josiah leapt from the road and into the marsh. Mud sucked at his legs and he pulled his knees high and kept running. From behind him came the shouts, "Whoa, there! Whoa, there!" It was the demanding voice of a Putnam—Edward, Thomas, Nathaniel, John—it didn't matter which one. If any of them caught him . . .

Josiah hurled himself through the marsh. Once on high ground, he crawled on his belly until he was sure no one had followed him. But there was no time to stop. He had to find Oneko and the widow.

Would Oneko know where to go? He had only been as far as the Hutchinson fields and then from another direction. Would he march right up to the house if he could find it and deposit the widow on the doorstep?

Or would they both be too frightened and head back for Topsfield?

Josiah pulled himself up from the ground and ran. His boots were heavy with mud and dragged at the ground like lead weights, but he pumped on toward the road, across it, and into the trees. Ahead of him the Meeting House sat sternly in the dark. Just within sight were the lights in his own windows.

"Oneko!" Josiah whispered. His only answer was the pounding rain. He didn't dare call louder. Whatever Putnam it was who'd spotted him was probably still pacing the road looking for him with his crown lantern.

Josiah patted his waist for his pouch and then punched himself. It was empty. He'd given one whistle to Oneko and didn't have his new one with him. Then like a startled chicken, Josiah scratched at the ground and came up with a broad blade of grass. It was slick with rain, but with trembling fingers he pinched it between his thumbs and blew. Nothing happened.

"Come on, then!" he hissed to it. Again he pinched it and, closing his eyes, put it to his lips. A thin wail pierced the night.

He blew again—once, twice, three times. He saw movement ahead in the shadows, and he squinted through the rain to see better.

The Meeting House door was opening.

Josiah leaped behind a tree, heart hammering. But he heard no sound of footsteps. Just silence. And then, a note—strong and sure from a wooden whistle. Josiah peeked out. There in the shadows of the Meeting House crouched Oneko, with the widow neatly tucked onto his back.

"The Lord provides shelter," the widow said happily when Josiah was once more trotting beside them.

"There!" Josiah said. "There is my house!"

But Oneko was already up the path as if he had been there in his mind a thousand times before.

As soon as Josiah opened the front door, relief flooded over him. He had never thought he would be happy to hear the sound of Hope's rattled breathing. But his relief came to an end when his father burst into the hall. His eyes were the eyes of a man with nothing to do with his fear but shake it—hard.

"Where have you been?" his voice thundered. "It's not enough we have your sister dyin'—but you have to go runnin' off like a—"

He stopped as his eyes found the Indian boy, dripping on the plank floor with a wispy old woman on his back.

"What—"

"Papa." Josiah stepped aside. "This is the Widow Hooker, from Topsfield. She's friend to me, and to Hope. She can heal her—she can cure her, I know it!"

Voices began to stir from the kitchen. The Porters and Elizabeth Proctor and the rest.

"Joseph, is it Josiah?"

Josiah worked hard to get his mouth to move. "Please let her help us, Papa! I know she's a—"

"A friend," the widow said quietly.

But Papa was looking hard at Oneko. The Indian's eyes darted wildly; he looked like a wolf caught in a farmer's trap. Always so free, now so trapped, and so afraid.

"He'd best be gone," Joseph Hutchinson said.

And before they could turn their heads, he was.

Four pairs of cautious eyes fell on the Widow Hooker when she entered the Hutchinsons' kitchen. But *her* eyes went to Hope, who looked more shriveled than ever. The widow took a step toward her, then stopped and lifted her whiskery chin.

"I am Faith Hooker," she said to the group. "I am friend to Josiah and to Hope. I have a healing gift from the Lord, and Josiah has asked me to come here and share it with Hope."

She looked directly at Joseph Hutchinson. "I will do what I can, but only with your permission, sir."

All eyes except Josiah's shifted to the master of the house. Josiah kept watching the widow. She was a stranger in a town where people thought they had the right to throw her in jail because she didn't practice Christianity the way they did. But she wasn't afraid at all. She knew whose side God was on.

"Dr. Griggs has tried many things," said Josiah's father. "None have worked."

"I'm sure I would have tried those things first as well." The widow put her basket on the table. "These are treatments I have learned from my Indian friends."

Josiah heard someone gasp, and the widow smiled. "They are not magic spells and witch doctor brews, Mr. Hutchinson. They are simply herbs and roots we can all grow and pick. Most people just haven't learned from our Indian friends what to do with them yet. God has led me to them." She nodded toward the basket. "Here they are."

A gray, mouselike voice spoke then from beside the fire. "Please, Joseph. Let her try."

Mama, so small and quiet, had spoken up against a room full of doubters. Her husband looked at her long and hard.

"God be with you then," he said finally. "What do you need?"

"Clean linens and some freshly boiled water."

Mama staggered to her feet, but the widow put up a tiny, elfin hand. "Goody Hutchinson, you look mighty ill yourself. Lie down, eh? Josiah can help me. He has been my assistant before."

All eyes stared at Josiah in surprise, but he ignored them. There was work to be done. There was his sister to save.

Water was boiled and Hope was wrapped in clean linens, while out of the basket came purple flowers Josiah recognized as Queen-of-the-Meadow, and meadowsweet, and the bark, leaves and roots of a poplar and a willow tree.

"These will break the fever," the widow told Josiah as she bent over the pot. "Later, when she can chew, we'll have her nibble on the bark of the cinchona tree there. Next, we'll work on that cough with some Indian turnip root and poke-wood berries."

Hope's clogged breathing rattled on and the widow shook her head.

"Is it too late?" Josiah whispered.

"It may be too late for my work," she said, "but it's never too late for God's."

When all was ready, the widow sat on the bed beside Hope and lifted her gently from the pillows. The tiny woman suddenly looked strong to Josiah, and even Hope's painful breathing seemed to relax against her.

"God's own Hope," she said in her raspy voice. "The Lord has sent me with sweet drink. Can you sip now?"

Hope only moaned.

"Fetch me a spoon, Josiah," the widow said.

As everyone watched in silence, Josiah produced a spoon. Slowly, patiently, the widow dipped it into the sweet-smelling broth and let the drops fall into Hope's mouth. She moaned again, but then her tongue appeared, and she licked her lips.

"There's a sign of life, praise God," the widow said. She

seemed to be talking only to Hope, and suddenly Josiah felt as if he were outside a special circle. He moved to the table where Goody Proctor, Goody Porter, and Goody Hutchinson sat and watched in wonder. His head felt heavy, and he let it drop to his arms on the table top. His eyelids had barely begun to droop when the iron knocker fell heavily against the front door.

"'Tis Reverend Parris," Goodman Porter reported from the window.

A chill fell over the kitchen when Reverend Parris came in. Only the widow was undisturbed. She kept talking softly to Hope and spooning medicine between her lips.

"I came as soon as I received the news," Reverend Parris said to Goodman Hutchinson. "I was in a meeting with—" His glance shot around the room and he bit his lip. If eyes met his at all, they were cold. "Has she gone to the arms of the Lord yet?"

"No!"

"Josiah!" His mother put her hand on his arm. He didn't realize he'd spoken, or that he'd scraped his chair back and stood with his chin tilted at the minister.

There was a shocked silence. Josiah breathed hard and waited for someone to shout him out of the room.

"No, Reverend Parris," said Josiah's father instead. "We've one last hope in Goodwife Hooker."

Reverend Parris stared blankly at the widow with a face that didn't know her.

"Good evening, Reverend," the widow said. And she kept spooning.

The minister edged closer to her and peered into the cup

she held. "You're not from Salem Village."

Josiah's father sighed loudly. "We have hard sickness here, Reverend Parris, and much sorrow in the house. What have you come for?"

Reverend Parris turned his pinched face toward Papa's. "I've come to pray with you—you and your wife. You refuse to support my ministry here, but it is my ministry nonetheless. Your daughter is a Christian girl, and she deserves my prayers and those of the church."

There was a long silence. Josiah waited for his father to usher Reverend Parris to the door, perhaps even by his shiny black collar. But Joseph Hutchinson searched his face carefully, and said, "Good, then."

No! Josiah wanted to shout. But heads bowed and the Reverend Parris prayed over Hope while the Widow Hooker finished spooning. She nodded at his words now and then and followed his prayer with a raspy "Amen."

When he finished, the Reverend Parris picked up his hat from the table and surveyed the room with his eyes. They stopped at the stack of books on the arm of Papa's chair.

"Mark this, Mr. Hutchinson," he said. "It's said you have some strange ideas. I have a notion they come from the reading of books other than the Bible. A Christian needs no more than the Scripture. It's my duty as your minister to point out that the church frowns on laymen such as yourself clouding your minds with words that do not come from God, that do not improve our sinful nature and fill our minds with God's Holy Word."

"Everything good comes from God, Reverend Parris,"

Joseph Hutchinson said. "The Good Lord blessed me with a mind. I have a notion He intends for me to use it. Good evening, sir." And he stomped from the house.

Reverend Parris pinched his lips together and fumbled for his hat. He didn't say a word as he hurried out the door.

Goody Proctor followed him out, the Porters coming after them. Goody Hutchinson slumped wearily into her husband's chair and was asleep in moments.

"Josiah," said the widow, "lie you down on the settle."

"I am going to stay up and help you," he said stubbornly. But he stretched out and twitched around uneasily.

"Why did my father let that man pray over Hope?" he said fitfully. "My father hates—my father doesn't like him."

The widow looked up sharply. "Because Reverend Parris is a man of God, Josiah."

Josiah snorted.

"The people of Salem Village chose him to be their minister, and he was ordained in their church before God Himself. Whatever his shortcomings may be, he is one of God's messengers. His ideas are different from your father's, but his prayers go from his heart to God's."

Josiah sat up sharply. "But he's mean to children! He's even sometimes mean to the fathers and the mothers!"

"He's a human bein' with faults like the rest of us," the widow said. "But we've naught to judge him." She chuckled to herself. "I think he does the best he can."

Josiah lay down stiffly. It would take some thinking to sort that out—and he was too tired now. Even as he blinked against sleep, it took him over.

When he awoke, the mid-morning sun was shooting through the diamond panes, but the kitchen felt as if someone had just come in and said "Shhhh!"

Josiah's first thought took shape. *Hope.*

He scrambled from the settle and fell at the side of her bed. He couldn't hear her breathing rattle.

He pulled the linens from around her face, and her black eyes fluttered open for a tiny instant. Soft, soundless breath puffed from her nose, and she slept peacefully.

The door opened and the widow came in, her basket overflowing.

"She's well!" Josiah cried.

"Hush! She's needin' real sleep now. She's around the bend, but she's not home yet."

Josiah hurried to the window. Ninny and her mother were already in the pasture while the chickens pecked busily at seed on the ground.

"My work!" he cried. "Is Mama out there doin' it?"

The widow tossed her head back and laughed. "Your mama is up in her bed asleep, and she won't be comin' down for some time now. She's ill herself." She cleared her throat as she poured a cup of cider into a mug and offered it to Josiah.

He shook his head. "I have to get dressed. Papa will be waitin' with my work!"

Even as he spoke, his father's big form filled the doorway, and Josiah shrank back. His punishment was sure to come sooner or later.

But his father padded quietly to the cot and looked down at Hope. "My daughter is much improved since you come," he told the widow. "My wife and I would be grateful if you would stay until she's up and well."

Josiah's mouth fell open.

"I must see to my house, Mr. Hutchinson," she said. "Josiah came to me in such a hurry, I hadn't time to—"

"Josiah and I can take the wagon up and bring whatever you need. You tell us what you want done while we're there, and we'll see to it."

Josiah stared at his father in disbelief, but the widow nodded, as if she had expected him to say that all along.

"We've much to be thankful to you for," he said.

"God works through His people," she said.

And a thin voice from the bed by the fire said, "Amen."

✢ ✢ ✢

few days later, Josiah and his father took the wagon to Topsfield, a list tucked safely into Josiah's head.

The widow's cabin seemed much smaller with his father in it. Joseph Hutchinson's big shoulders barely cleared the door.

While Josiah's papa stood in the center of the room, looking around, Josiah went to the window and tried to appear casual as he peered out. If he could just catch a glimpse of Oneko and know he was safe—

"A poor woman is Faith Hooker," his father said.

Josiah turned in surprise. "Is she?"

"There is naught to holler at here—save a table, a few chairs—" He stopped, and for the first time in a week, the hard lines on his face grew soft at the edges. "She's brought us great riches, though, has she not?"

"Aye," Josiah said.

"Come. Let's get what we've come for and be off now."

Josiah took the basket and went outside, muttering the widow's list to himself. *More Queen-of-the-Mountain. Indian turnip roots.*

Then Josiah heard a rustling from amid the stand of spruces. He dropped the basket and took a few steps forward.

"Oneko?" He glanced at the cabin. Through the window he saw his father moving around. "Oneko!" he called out again. "My father is here. You'd best be gone. The widow will be back in a few days."

There was no answer. No straight brown body emerged from the trees. Instead, the branches of one spruce tree parted, just enough for a pair of black eyes to look through.

Josiah gasped and stepped back. The eyes went through him like an arrow, and then they were gone. Josiah blinked and squinted, but saw nothing now except the branches of the spruce, nervously swaying.

They were Indian eyes, for sure. But they weren't Oneko's.

"Josiah! Have you those simples?"

He snatched up the basket and headed for the wagon where he climbed up beside his father. He glanced toward the woods. All was still.

They were both quiet for a long time as they rocked and swayed their way home. The village was just coming into sight when Joseph Hutchinson said, "I should like to help the Widow Hooker somehow. Perhaps hire her to help your mother with some of the simpler chores, at least until Hope is fully well again." He cut a glance down at Josiah. "What say you?"

But before Josiah could answer, they were hailed from the
side of the road by a sharp voice from atop a horse.

"Whoa, there!" Edward Putnam cried. "Hutchinson, whoa,
there!"

"Doesn't the man ever work his fields?" Josiah's father
muttered. "Doesn't he have aught to do but watch my
comings and goings?" Sighing heavily he pulled the wagon to
a halt.

The deacon looked at them out of a very red face. "It is my
duty to remind you, Mr. Hutchinson," he said, "that tomorrow
is Thursday."

Josiah's father gave a hard laugh. "I'm grateful to you,
Putnam. Good day, then."

"Don't sport with me, Mister! You know Thursday is
Lecture Day, and we've not seen you in the church on a
Thursday in three months."

"And you won't," Goodman Hutchinson said wearily. "Now,
good day."

"Wait." Edward put his hand up importantly and moved
toward the wagon as if he were about to reveal a great secret.
Josiah clung to the seat to keep from leaning forward. "I've
something else to say. Reverend Parris has this morning told
us that you have a stranger staying under your roof. This
Hooker woman."

His father's hands clenched the reins. "Aye. And what law
of the church am I breakin' now, Putnam?"

"None, if like Reverend Parris, you were not aware that the
woman—" He glanced over both shoulders and continued in
a hoarse whisper, "The woman is a Quaker."

Josiah looked down at his hands and felt the fear creeping up from his toes.

"That makes her a heathen, Mr. Hutchinson. And yourself one, too, if you continue to harbor such—"

"Out of my way, Putnam. I've near to run over you before, and I'll be more careful about it this time!"

"I am not afeard of you, Hutchinson!" Edward cried. But he pulled his horse back from the wagon. As Josiah's father picked up the reins and the oxen started forward, Edward Putnam fired his parting words. "That isn't all, Mister! I'm to warn all citizens of Salem that an Indian's been sighted in the village."

Josiah jerked around in the seat. Putnam's eyes met his. "He was headin' up Wolf Pits Meadow when my brother Thomas spotted him. Thomas shot the savage—but he got away—disappeared through the marsh leavin' a trail of blood behind him. Mark it—and mind you keep your doors and windows bolted. The Indians will be back for revenge. He was a young one."

Both Josiah and his father sat like stones in the wagon, even after Edward Putnam tipped his beaver hat and trotted away. Without a word, Joseph Hutchinson clicked his tongue at the oxen, and the wagon lumbered toward the farm. Josiah stared straight ahead, but his heart was pounding.

Oneko. Of course it was Oneko. Josiah had told him not to come into the village. Shot! Shot—and now his family was looking for him. That was the answer to the eyes in the trees at the cabin.

When they reached the barn, Josiah hurled himself from the wagon and ran for the door.

"Josiah!" his father called.

Josiah stopped and clenched his fists to keep from screaming. *Yes, I brought an Indian into the village. But he isn't a savage. There was no need to shoot him.*

"Josiah," said his father quietly, "the Indians take care of their own. You've naught to worry over." He stepped past Josiah and out into the sunshine. As he went by, his hand gently brushed Josiah's shoulder. "Get you in now. The widow will be needin' your help."

The widow was putting a handful of the first wildflowers into a mug on the table when Josiah came in. Cornbread was baking and soup was brewing and the air in the kitchen was cheerful. With the widow moving about, chatting to herself in her dry-leaf voice, it felt as if they were in the cabin in Topsfield.

Josiah set the basket on the table and straightened his shoulders.

"Ah, good messenger from the hills, eh?" she said. She smiled her twinkly smile. "There's someone to see you, there by the fire."

"I must tell you—"

"Go now!"

With a sigh, Josiah tiptoed over to Hope's cot and peeked. Her cheeks were still as white as the linens wrapped around her, but her breathing was smooth and even.

"She is awake," the widow said.

Josiah leaned in close. "Hope?" he said softly.

"There's no need to whisper." The widow chuckled. "She won't break."

"Hope!"

Her eyes fluttered open. "Speak up, brainless boy. I'm not an invalid." Her voice was thin like a curl of smoke, but it was there.

Josiah broke into a grin. "You're well!"

"They say you've been doing all my work for me," she went on, as if he hadn't spoken.

Josiah shrugged. "Not the spinning."

She closed her eyes and smiled a gray smile. "I'll be up leading you on a merry chase again before summer comes. Of course, there's no fun in it now. You know where I go."

"Then you can all come and we'll make celebration together," the widow said. "Hope and Sarah and Rachel, Josiah—and Oneko. He's part of our family, eh?"

Josiah looked down at his hands. It was so peaceful in the kitchen, so happy—the way it was in the widow's cabin. He couldn't tell them now about Oneko, or it would all slide out between the cracks around the window panes and the light would go out in the kitchen.

The Indians take care of their own, his father had said. Even now they probably had him in a bed like Hope. And his father or brother or uncle had only gone to the cabin to tell the widow he was fine.

"You're so serious, boy," Hope said.

"Be serious about your work then," said the widow. "This girl must rest. Go and take this broth to your mother. And here—" She put the mug of flowers on the wooden tray. "She'll be needin' these, eh?"

For the next few days, Josiah worked hard. He had his own chores to do, and Hope's, and when he had a free moment he helped the widow prepare the medicines for his sister and ran broth and tea up the stairs to his mother. The Widow Hooker was beginning to look gray and tired, and many of her conversations with Hope were exchanges of coughing. She had helped them so much, it felt good to tell her to rest by the fire while he fetched the fresh linens and pulled more turnip roots.

In fact, many things felt good, and they all helped drive the fears about Oneko from his mind. *The Indians take care of their own,* he told himself over and over. *And I will take care of my own.* He didn't say a word to the widow or Hope about their Indian friend.

One morning as Josiah brought the eggs to the kitchen, he saw Sarah Proctor and Rachel Porter standing on tiptoes outside the widow and peering in.

"Hope's there by the fire," Josiah told them.

"We see her," Rachel said. "We've been tapping on the window, but she won't turn 'round."

Josiah slapped his palm against the glass, but Hope sat with her back to them, propped against her pillows and working on her sampler.

"The girl's deaf!" Rachel said.

They followed Josiah inside, and Hope's face lit up when she saw them in the doorway.

"Rachel! Sarah!" she cried.

"You're so pale—"

"And so thin—"

"They told us you might die—"

Josiah awkwardly set the eggs on the table and turned to make a run for it. He always felt clumsy and red-faced in a room full of loud, squealing girls.

"There's no need to whisper," Hope said.

Josiah stopped.

"Girl, you *are* deaf!" Rachel said.

Laughing like howling wolves, Rachel and Sarah began to shout at Hope. Josiah slammed the door behind him and ran for the field.

"What are you running from, Big Squirrel?"

The Widow Hooker was in the herb garden, tidying up the scattered plants. Josiah stopped at the little gate.

"Girls," he said.

She coughed and caught her breath. "And what more?"

"And—nothing more."

"I've never known you to be afraid of girls or much of anything—except things you don't want to know, eh?"

"Is Hope deaf now?" he blurted out.

The widow was still for a moment, and then slowly she nodded. "We cannot blink it, Josiah. I think the fever has left her with somewhat less hearing than she had before."

Josiah shook his head as if to do so would change the truth. "But she had the sharpest ears in Salem Village!"

The widow paused for a moment before she spoke. "Once Hope told me that when you were small she used to talk for you. She was your mouth." She rocked her head from side to side. "Now you must be her ears."

Josiah felt suddenly as if he were sinking in mud that

would soon suck him into the ground completely. "Why? Why does God do that?"

The widow leaned forward and shook her head. "We cannot question God, Josiah. We can only give thanks."

"Thanks? That she can barely hear?"

"Thanks—that she's alive."

Josiah felt his cheeks fill up with color, and he hung his head. The widow coughed hard and put out her hand. "No shame, no shame. Help me sit down, please, Big Squirrel. I've a need to rest, eh?"

Together they sat on the ground amid the herbs. Josiah waited for her to catch her breath.

"Hope will be completely well very soon," she said finally. "Your mother is up and about, too. It's time I went back home and tended to my own life."

"But you're staying here!" Josiah said. "Didn't Papa ask you?"

"Aye."

"Then you must stay!"

The widow choked happily on a laugh. "Joseph Hutchinson is *your* papa, not mine. The Widow Hooker takes care of her own life, eh?"

Josiah felt the mud seeping in all around him as she went on. "Your father was a brave man to even ask me, but I cannot stay here and have the villagers pointin' their fingers at him and worse, because I'm livin' under his roof. I've asked him to take me home today."

"Nay!"

"Big Squirrel." Her voice was quiet but firm. "God has a

path for me. It's up there in Topsfield, not here." She patted his hand. "And what of those summer days when all of us will gather on the grass in the meadow and eat the berries, eh? You and Hope and Oneko—"

Josiah shook his head and pulled himself up from the mud. "What is it, Big Squirrel?"

But Josiah didn't answer. There was nothing to say.

It was almost dark when Josiah's father hitched two of the oxen to the wagon. He and the widow had decided at dinner that it would be best for everyone if they traveled at night, away from the prying eyes of the villagers. The widow had spent the afternoon giving Josiah's mother instructions for Hope's medicine and tidying up the kitchen. By the time Papa brought the wagon around to the house, she was tired and gray, and her coughing shook her little body so that she had to stop and clutch the table until she caught her breath.

Josiah heard and saw it all from outside the window where he was chopping wood. There was plenty of wood for the rest of the week, but he couldn't go inside. If he did, he would have to tell the widow that Oneko wasn't going to be there waiting for her.

"Your cough sounds just like Hope's," he heard his mother say. "Would it not be wise to stay just one more day and rest before you go home?"

"And miss seeing the first fawns appear in my woods?" The widow chuckled and then coughed. "I'd best be off tonight, Deborah. I feel it."

Goodman Hutchinson carried out the basket and the

Widow Hooker's other belongings, and Hope and her mother waved from the window as the widow followed him down the path. Josiah thought he was well hidden at the corner of the house, but his father looked right at him.

"Josiah—are you comin'?"

The widow turned and looked around.

Josiah's stomach grew tight, and it hurt to hold back the tears. She was going back to a dark, empty cabin, not knowing that Oneko wouldn't be there. She should stay here, where all of them could be happy. But she couldn't, because of them—the Putnams and Reverend Parris and the rest. He didn't care whether it was right or not—he hated them. And in a small way, he hated his father for letting them drive her away. He shook his head.

"Come then, Faith," said his father, "let me help you."

Josiah's father leaned down from the wagon to catch hold of her arms. But as if she were suddenly grabbed and shaken by an invisible hand, the widow began to cough, violently, and she didn't stop. Gasping for air, she slipped from Papa's grasp. Before he could catch her, she'd fallen to the ground in a tiny gray pile.

✠ ⁃✛⁃ ✠

Chapter Sixteen

ore broth, Josiah! Quickly now!"

Josiah splashed the yellow liquid into the mug and handed it back to Hope. "Do you think we put enough turnip root in it?" he asked.

There was no answer.

"Hope!" Josiah wiggled her arm. She looked at him and studied his lips. "Do you think we put enough turnip root in it?"

She frowned for a moment, then nodded. "I did it just the way she showed Mama. We'll make her well, Josiah. We *will.*"

She tilted her chin and Josiah nodded. But he wasn't sure. Lying on Hope's cot, twisting with pain and groping for breath, the widow didn't look as if she would ever be well.

Papa had carried her from the wagon and put her on the cot, and Hope and her mother had set about making more of the same medicines she had brewed for Hope. The four of them worked until almost midnight to break the fever. When finally the sweat poured from the Widow Hooker and she lay still and cool, Mama fell asleep on the settle, and Papa dozed fitfully in the chair by the window.

Now the widow shook her head, and Hope let the medicine run gently down the pillows.

"That's enough for now," Hope said to the widow. "You get so tired, even from sipping. Sleep now."

But the Widow Hooker shook her head and motioned them closer.

"You don't need me," she said as they leaned in. The leaves in her voice were brittle.

"What did she say?" Hope said.

"Aye, we *do* need you here!" Josiah cried. "Everything is right when you're with us. It's cheerful and—"

"You have a good, sweet mother," she said. "She is quiet, but she is wise. She saves her strength for the real battles."

Hope clutched the covers in frustration and looked from Josiah to the widow and back again. "What does she *say*?" she asked.

As loudly as he could without waking his parents, Josiah repeated it for her. The widow waited, pulling at the air for breath.

"Your papa is strong," she went on. "And God is strong with him. He is not like these others—Putnam and Porter—"

"Porter?" Josiah shook his head. "The Porters are our friends!"

"Your papa is honest. He lives a life of truth. Don't be afeard of him. It's a good man. The village is changing and he will need your help. You must respect him, no matter what happens."

She was seized by a fit of coughing that seemed to shake loose her bones. Hope grabbed at the covers and held her until she stopped.

"You have a good family here," she said in a voice even Josiah could hardly hear. "It's this village with its dark people that tears the light from your house. But it will come back. You children—you must help bring the light—"

She trailed off. Hope grabbed her and sat her up. "No! No!"

"I am here, God's own Hope," the widow said. "But I must rest now. Tell Oneko."

Her eyes closed and Hope held her face close to her mouth.

"She's breathing," Josiah said. "I can hear her breathing."

Hope rested her head beside the widow, and for a minute Josiah thought she had gone to sleep, too. He would have to stay awake all night and spoon the broth in whenever the widow awoke.

But suddenly Hope sat up. "Tomorrow you must find Oneko and tell him."

"Tell him what?" Josiah said uneasily.

"That she is ill. That she's here with us. He'll be looking for her."

Josiah swallowed hard. "No, he won't."

"Why not?" Her eyes narrowed. "Why not, Josiah?"

"Because—because—he was shot here in the village by Thomas Putnam that night we brought her here. He got away—"

To his surprise, she didn't cry out. Her face grew soft. "He was trying to save my life," Hope said. "That's the second time."

Josiah sat up straight. "The second time?"

Her pale cheeks turned pink. "The first time I met him, last summer, he fished me out of the river. I fell in trying to follow you—and I would have drowned if he hadn't found me. After that, he always seemed to be wherever I was, like he was watching over me."

"He pulled me out of the river, too!" Josiah said. "Didn't the widow tell you that?"

Hope shook her head. "I didn't even know you knew her. I didn't follow you up there that day. I had gone up there to visit her myself."

"She never told you—anything?"

"Did she ever tell you anything about me?"

Josiah shook his head.

Hope smiled down at the gray little elfin woman who struggled on the cot between them. "She is your friend, and she is my friend. To her, we are real people, and separate people."

Hope put her head on the edge of the cot and Josiah did the same. It felt warm and for the moment safe. God suddenly seemed close.

Please take care of your own, Josiah whispered.

He was awake before dawn, and he bolted up from the floor and looked around. The chair was empty. His mother slept on the settle, and Hope was sitting up, holding the widow's hand.

Josiah scrambled to his feet. "Do you want me to get some broth?"

Hope shook her head. "She won't need any, Josiah." She

paused. "She's gone."

The front door opened, but Josiah kept his eyes glued to the widow's face, waiting for her to open her twinkling eyes and say, "And what would you be lookin' at, Big Squirrel?" *Wake up!* he wanted to shout at her. *Wake up! There are still things you haven't told me!*

"Wake up."

Josiah jumped. Joseph Hutchinson bent over his wife on the settle. "Wake up. And Hope—you dress yourself warm now. Josiah, fetch more blankets."

"Joseph?" Mama sat up sleepily.

"The widow has died, Deborah," he said simply. "I think it best we take her up to her cabin and bury her there before there's light in the sky. We don't want any of these stiff-necked people to discover us, eh?"

"You'll dig her grave alone?" Goody Hutchinson said.

"I've gone to John Proctor's already. He's come to help us." He stopped and his eyes went to Josiah. "And we have Josiah. We should do well, then."

And so that morning they put the widow Faith Hooker to rest. Under the cover of a gray spring mist, Joseph Hutchinson carried her body to the wagon wrapped in blankets as if she were merely being taken back home. But as they slipped out of the village and wound their way along the back roads toward Topsfield, Josiah knew, as clearly as he'd ever known anything, that when they arrived she would not wake up and greet her cabin with a raspy chuckle. She would not hurry to the edge of the woods to check on the deer. And she would not answer any of his questions—or Hope's—never, never again. It hurt him as nothing ever had before.

Where are you God? Josiah had prayed—but He, like the Widow Hooker, was gone.

Hope was allowed to choose the spot for the grave, and she picked a place just at the edge of the spruce trees. "She will feel the deer playing above her," she whispered to Josiah.

The sun cast a glow the color of apple blossoms on the tops of the hills when Josiah and his father and John Proctor finished covering the Widow Hooker's body in the grave they'd dug for her. The white linen Hope and her mother had wrapped her in slowly disappeared under the shovels of dirt until only a smooth mound remained in front of them. The hurt grew in Josiah's chest.

"Shall we pray?" Papa said.

They gathered in a knot against the chill of the spring dawn, and Joseph Hutchinson's quiet voice settled over them.

"Heavenly Father," he said, "I am no minister. But as your child here on earth, I commend to You another of Your children. We have done all we can to care for her. We now lift her up to Your everlasting arms, where by Your grace she can live in eternity with You and her loved ones."

"Abraham Hooker," Hope whispered.

What about her loved ones here? Josiah thought. But he said nothing.

A heavy silence lowered on them.

"Faith's things," Mama said. "Is there anyone, any relative to come and fetch them from the cabin?"

"No!" Josiah cried. Hope tugged at his sleeve, a question

in her eyes. "They want someone to come and take her belongings!" he shouted to her.

Hope tilted her chin. "She would want the cabin left as it is, I'm sure. There are just a few things—may we stay and collect them?" She nudged Josiah with her elbow. "We can walk home then, eh?"

Josiah nodded.

"It's too far!" Mama said. "And Hope not fully well—"

"It appears they have both done it before, does it not?" their father said.

Josiah looked at the ground, but he felt Hope stand tall beside him.

"We never meant to deceive you, Papa," she said. "But she was a good friend. We saw nothing wrong in that. We will take our punishment, but please let us do this for her."

Now Josiah nudged his sister. He wasn't interested in taking any punishment. The empty ache inside him was worse than a whipping.

"Good, then," Papa said. "Josiah, you are to take care of your sister, d'y'hear? And you're both to be home to help your mother with the dinner and me with the chores."

Once the wagon left with Papa and Mama and John Proctor rocking in the seats, an uneasy quiet dropped over the cabin and its little yard. It was as if the widow had taken the life of it with her. His feet as heavy as bags of mud, Josiah followed Hope inside.

Hope sat down at the table and ran her hand over its worn, smooth top. Josiah could almost see the memories of afternoons spent there racing through her eyes.

Josiah squatted at the hearth. The stones that once felt so warm against his back the day he'd lain there soaking wet were now cold.

"She wouldn't want people comin' in here and taking her belongings," Hope said suddenly.

"They aren't hers anymore."

"Josiah!"

"No—not because she's—dead. But—without her here—they just aren't the same. They don't have—the light in them."

Hope stared at him, almost as if she were seeing someone else. Slowly, she nodded. "She said *we* must bring back the light. Do you remember that?"

"Aye."

Tears shone in Hope's eyes, but she smiled. "Perhaps she meant for *us* to have this place, Josiah!"

"Us?"

"Aye. A place to come to, like we always did when she was here—only now we have to bring our own light."

"Would we tell anyone?" Josiah said.

Hope's face grew serious. "Mama and Papa. We've naught to lie to them anymore, Josiah, and keep things from them. The widow said we must respect them no matter what happens."

"What do you think is going to happen in the village?" Josiah said.

"I don't know. I only know we have to help—eh?"

The cabin grew quiet again. Josiah sighed against the pain in his chest. It still hurt. But there was something comforting about the talking and the deciding of things. There was the hurt, but not the muddy feeling.

Josiah quietly shut the cabin door behind them, and they tiptoed carefully past the grave on their way to the woods.

"Good-bye, widow," Hope said.

Josiah stopped and hunched his neck to see into the trees. "I saw something move," he whispered.

"Josiah, you know I can't hear you—"

"Shhhh!"

Josiah squinted through the spruce. A branch moved, and a pair of piercing brown eyes squinted back. They were the same eyes he'd seen the day he was here with his father.

Beside him, Hope gasped. Her hand slid into Josiah's and squeezed tight.

"Who is it?" she whispered.

Josiah shook his head and waited, frozen. Slowly, the branches separated, and Hope wrung Josiah's fingers.

Emerging through the trees was the stern brown face of an Indian man.

✠ ⸭ ✠

Chapter Seventeen

Hope and Josiah could no more turn and run than could the trees. Even as the Indian strode toward them, they stood rooted to the ground.

"Josiah!" Hope hissed huskily. Her grip threatened to squeeze his fingers off his hand.

The Indian stopped a foot away, tall and straight-legged. His eyes looked down on them the way Thomas Putnam's often did—as if he were bothered by their being there and wanted to be done with them as quickly as possible.

Without even a grunt he reached down and grabbed both their wrists with one hand. Their hands were forced together like two frightened rabbits squeezed into the same trap. He turned and walked back to the woods in long, angry strides. Hope and Josiah tumbled, terrified, behind him. Hope screamed, and Josiah pulled at his wrist, but the Indian's fingers were like bands of steel. He strode into the trees, pushing aside branches that came back to slap them in the face.

"Where are you taking us?" Hope cried.

For answer, the Indian flung them forward and let go. They rolled onto a carpet of ferns at the foot of a pine tree, almost into the lap of another Indian.

Josiah scrambled to sit up.

"Oneko!" Hope cried.

But Oneko's eyes were guarded as he looked first at Hope, then at Josiah.

"Your leg!" Hope said.

Josiah looked down at the strong brown leg, now propped on a blanket and wrapped in what looked like wet tobacco leaves. Hope reached down and softly touched the wound. Josiah winced and then, with a growl, the tall Indian yanked her shoulder and she fell back onto the ground. He spat out a string of words that sent her rushing to Josiah's side.

Oneko spoke then. His voice was timid, and Josiah saw fear in his eyes as he looked at the other Indian. Was this Oneko's father? Josiah had a sudden vision of being dragged to an Indian camp and tied to a stake over an open fire—

Oneko's father stepped back and folded his arms, still glaring at them.

"I think he's giving us one chance to explain," Josiah said to Hope. "It's best you do it."

Hope's face was ash-colored but she tilted her chin and turned to Oneko. "You know that we are your friends. We have naught to hurt you—you have saved our lives! Mine twice!"

Josiah found himself nodding violently.

"The person who shot you—he is from our village. But we are not like him. He—"

Hope stopped. Oneko was frowning and shaking his head, as if his thoughts, too, were mired in mud.

Oneko's father snarled at him and jabbed his finger toward Hope and Josiah. Hope bit her lip and stepped back.

"I think we should run," she said.

But Josiah's legs wouldn't move. He could only stare at Oneko, who for the first time was more helpless than he was. Josiah knew what to say. He knew how to make it right. But as always the words were knotted and tangled. Hope tugged at his hand.

"Please—we must go!" she said.

But Josiah pulled away. He took a long breath and tilted his chin. "The man who shot you hates the things he doesn't understand. But we don't hate you. We understand."

The woods were quiet. Oneko sat back against the pine tree. For a tiny second, the warm returned to his eyes.

And then Oneko's father let out a low growl. Hope shrank back against Josiah. Slowly, the tall Indian raised his arm and pointed toward the edge of the trees.

"He wants us to leave," Hope said. She began to back away.

"Wait," Josiah said. "We have to tell him—the widow told us to tell him."

Hope gritted her teeth. "Josiah—please—"

Oneko's father edged forward, still growling in his throat.

"Come, Josiah!" Hope said.

"No." Josiah lifted his chin once again. "Oneko, you have to know. The Widow Hooker—she died this morning. Your medicines saved Hope, but they couldn't save her."

A cry came from Oneko's lips that stopped them all. Even his father stood still and stunned.

"It hurts, Oneko!" For the first time Josiah knew what the pain was in his chest. It came from holding back the tears he wanted so much to cry. Because now it didn't hurt anymore. Now he was crying.

Hope tugged at his arm. "Come, Josiah."

The tears were almost blinding him, but Josiah turned for one last look at Oneko. His eyes were black and shiny with tears of his own.

With trembling fingers, Josiah untied the leather pouch from his breeches and held it out to Oneko. *Remember me,* his face said.

Oneko took the pouch and held it in his hands, his fingers barely touching it.

I will never forget you, his face answered.

When they were far from the woods, Hope stopped running and leaned against a tree. Tears ran down her face and she sobbed and choked for air all at once. "We'll never see him again."

"Aye," said Josiah. He smeared his sleeve across his eyes. "But he understands now. He'll never hate us."

Hope tilted her chin up. "He understands because *you* explained it to him. You were brave—and I was proud you were my brother."

The walk back to the village was long and slow and quiet. Josiah was tired down to his bones, and from the way Hope trudged beside him, lost in her thoughts, he knew she must be, too.

But when they reached the top of Thorndike Hill, Hope gasped and grabbed Josiah's arm.

"Look!" she cried.

Josiah's eyes searched below where she pointed. At the side of the road stood their two oxen, still hitched to the Hutchinson wagon.

They tore down the hill to the wagon, but it was empty, and no one was around.

"It doesn't look as if they were stuck," Hope said.

"Listen!"

"What?"

From the direction of the Meeting House came a tangle of voices, all shouting at once.

"There's trouble," Josiah said. "This way!"

He grabbed Hope's hand and together they rounded the curve and ran past Captain Walcott's and the parsonage. A crowd was gathered at the Meeting House, and amid the shouting it moved as if it were being pushed and shoved in all directions.

"They're tryin' to put someone in the stocks!" A cold fear gripped Josiah.

"Oh, Josiah!" Hope slowed to a halt and pulled on his arm. "Josiah—it's Papa."

"They've been harborin' a heathen!" someone yelled as Hope and Josiah burst into the circle. Mama saw them and flung her arms around both of them. Her body was shaking with crying.

"They're heathens themselves!"

"They've not given a penny to this church—"

"He deliberately tried to run over one of my pigs with his wagon—"

"He tried to run me down with his wagon—"

"I caught their boy tearin' down my fence—"

"Their habits are a danger to us all! We must protect this village!"

"Aye! God has given it to us—it must be saved!"

Josiah watched in horror as Willard, the grim-faced deputy constable, curled his fingers around Joseph Hutchinson's collar and flung him toward the stocks. Constable Cheever did the same to John Proctor. Goodman Hutchinson caught his balance and turned, his arms tightened and his fists clenched. The lines cut his face, and Josiah clutched hard at his mother's skirt. Fire came into his father's eyes and its heat pushed the circle backward.

"God have mercy on your soul, Willard!" Joseph Hutchinson shouted. "For if you do this, you'll need His mercy!"

"You take the Lord's name in vain!" cried a pinched voice.

Reverend Parris stood on the steps of the Meeting House, flanked by Putnams, who seemed to pinch him in further and hold him up.

For a moment there was a respectful hush as all eyes turned to the minister.

"I don't want this, Mr. Hutchinson!" Reverend Parris said. "But you leave me no choice!"

"It's the Putnams who leave you no choice!" Joseph

Hutchinson said. "I'd be willin' to be put in the stocks for God—I'll be whipped for Him! I'll be jailed. But I will not suffer punishment for the Putnams! All the Putnams can do is hate."

The crowd roared like one person, and as Josiah stared in disbelief, a sea of hands tore and groped and carried Papa and John Proctor toward the stocks.

"You'll never get my father in there!" Josiah cried. But his voice was lost in the shouting and he could only watch while Willard and Cheever pinned his father's great, strong arms behind him. The crowd quieted as the wooden jaws of the stockade clamped down over his wrists.

Above the hush came the sound of horses' hooves.

All heads turned. Through the crowd Josiah could only see a high black hat and a trail of silver hair.

"'Tis Israel Porter!" Mama said.

"Whoa, there!" the old man shouted, as much to the crowd as to his horse, Josiah thought. His handsome grandson climbed down from his horse and helped Mr. Porter to the ground. The crowd parted as the silvery old man made his way to the stockade. Giles followed, a smile playing at the corners of his mouth, as if he already knew the ending to this scene.

"We've hard business here, Israel Porter," Thomas Putnam said. "Please to keep the quiet and let us be about it."

"What business is it, puttin' innocent men in the stocks?" Mr. Porter said.

"Innocent? Joseph Hutchinson's been keepin' a Quaker in his home!" Nathaniel Putnam's shrill voice piped up.

"Do you know of the Declaration King James issued three years ago, Mr. Putnam?" Israel said.

Nathaniel sputtered.

"No," Israel Porter answered for him. "Because you're so busy sticking your nose into the business of others, you haven't time to look at what is going on in the world around you." Israel turned to the crowd and spoke in a warm voice. "King James made it law. All of his subjects everywhere have the freedom to worship as they wish. By that same law, then, Mr. Hutchinson has the right to associate himself with anyone of any faith he chooses. If he chooses to bring a good Samaritan into his home, so be it." He turned back to Nathaniel. "You do know about the good Samaritan, do you not? A woman who would come into a man's home and save his child is a good Samaritan. A man who would pass a family in distress on the Ipswich Road is not."

Nathaniel's wide face turned crimson, and the crowd muttered amongst itself.

"You cannot run Joseph Hutchinson out of this village the way you did George Burroughs," Israel Porter went on, "because he had a heart and a mind wider than anything you narrow-minded people could dream of!" His voice shook a little, and Giles touched his elbow gently.

Thomas Putnam broke through with a waving finger. "And what of the taxes they owe for the runnin' of the church and Reverend Parris's salary? That's still the law, Mister!"

The crowd came alive again, but Israel Porter calmly held up his hand. From it swung a leather pouch. "And if these taxes you speak of were paid, Mr. Hutchinson and Mr. Proctor would be allowed to go free, would they not?"

Thomas Putnam gave a hard laugh, but it was Reverend Parris who spoke. "I do not want it said that I am not a fair man!" he said, his voice teetering. "If the money is paid, surely the men will go free. But I do not think—"

"Mr. Willard," Israel Porter said quietly.

John Willard waved his hand in a weary motion.

Israel held out the leather pouch. "Mr. Willard, you will want to count this, but I assure you the money owed by Mr. Hutchinson and Mr. Proctor is all there—not a penny less." He put his hand on Willard's shoulder. "But perhaps you should set them free before you commence counting, eh?"

The crowd murmured like a disappointed child. The Putnams continued to cry out in protest, Reverend Parris disappeared into the Meeting House, and the rest of the villagers took their leave in scattered clumps.

"Come, children." Her head bowed, Mama put her arm around Hope's shoulder, and they hurried toward the farm.

But Josiah couldn't hurry—a muddy, disappointed feeling dragged at his feet.

His father stood up from the stocks and rubbed his wrists. His face was red and confused.

"Israel, I—"

"Hush, now!" said the old man. "We'd best not talk here. Shall we go to your house, perhaps for a cup of cider? What say you?"

Joseph Hutchinson nodded, and Josiah knew it was only with the greatest effort that he held up his chin as he headed for the wagon.

Josiah ran to his side. "I can bring it home, Papa." He didn't say, *I don't want you to have to walk past all these people when you're ashamed.* But that was what he thought. His father must be so ashamed of what had just happened. Why had he allowed Israel Porter to pay his way? It wasn't that he didn't have the money. It was that he didn't believe in what the money was paying for. And neither did Israel Porter—or so he thought.

"Thank you," his father said. And with his eyes straight ahead he walked toward his farm.

As Josiah climbed into the wagon and clicked his tongue at the oxen, his mind went back to that day at Putnam's fence. It *was* Giles Porter. The face he saw from the hill that day matched the handsome, smiling one he'd seen today—and he was doing something Israel Porter claimed he didn't believe in. What was happening here? Were these the changes in Salem Village they'd all talked about?

It was sure he would never find out from his father or the other men. So much had changed, but he was still a brainless boy. He would never be included in the explanations. He would never be free of this muddy thinking that bogged him down.

He missed the Widow Hooker until it hurt.

When Josiah carried the wood inside for the dinner fire, the door to the best room was slightly open, and he could see the men with their cider, their heads bent in serious conversation. His father stood before the trestle table and Israel Porter sat on the settle in front of the fire with his son

Benjamin and John Proctor. Giles stood respectfully apart
beside the writing desk, lightly fingering the candle box and
the spice chest but listening carefully. With a sigh, Josiah
pushed open the kitchen door.

"Josiah?"

He turned around slowly. "I, sir?"

"Aye. Come here."

Josiah stood uncertainly in the doorway. "Do you need
more cider, sir?"

"Nay. I think it's best you hear this. Sit you down—and
please to keep the quiet."

Josiah stepped inside the room and watched his father,
searching for a clue on his lined face.

"Perhaps with your son here, you will be more reasonable,"
Israel Porter said.

Joseph Hutchinson slapped his hand impatiently on the
table. "There's naught to be reasonable about! I won't have
you payin' my taxes for me!"

Israel Porter smiled into his mug. "You can repay me today,
Hutchinson."

"Nay! Reverend Parris can repay you! I'll not have money
going in my name to anything having to do with this village."

"You know what we have set out to do. The Putnams
planned even before Samuel Parris came here that the man
should be in their pockets, doing things their way, cutting the
village off from the town, and with it any chance of growth.
And they are succeeding, Joseph! Who are the deacons, eh?
Edward Putnam and Walcott—a Putnam puppet. And who
stands on either side of the minister every time he appears?

Thomas and Nathaniel Putnam. I know not how and when they meet to work their persuasion on him, but they have managed."

Josiah felt his eyes widening. He knew exactly how and when. The scene on the corner of his own farm—the two figures bent together in the night—came sharply back to him.

"We cannot blink it, Joseph. You know that. You believe that this village can be a place of freedom—a place where God's blessings can come in abundance, do you not?"

"Aye," Joseph Hutchinson said softly.

"And you, John Proctor?"

"Aye."

"And how do you suggest we stand up for that—and continue our trade with the town—and insure the freedom of our children—with the two of you in the stocks, eh? You couldn't read your books and advise us as you do—"

"Ach!" Josiah's father scraped his chair back and went to the window. "We'd have only been there a short time—"

"Until your taxes were paid. And you were able to defend yourself against keepin' a Quaker in your house."

"Friend," Mr. Hutchinson said stubbornly.

"Y'see? You'd have never defended yourself, and who was to do it for you?" The old man cackled. "Your boy here?"

His father's eyes settled on Josiah, and in that moment, a precious, silvery moment, Josiah saw him nod.

"You must trust me, all of you," Israel Porter went on. "It's God's work we do, and sometimes we must sacrifice our own pride to do His will."

They all fell silent. Even Giles Porter watched with a serious face. Joseph Hutchinson finally looked up from under his hooded brows.

"You are right, Israel," he said. "As always, you are right."

His hand reached out to clasp Israel Porter's, and a question faded from Josiah's mind. It had surely been Giles Porter who tore down Thomas Putnam's fence, and one thing was sure—Joseph Hutchinson had had no part in it. To tell him that perhaps Israel Porter had would be to slap his father in the face. Papa loved the old man—just as Josiah loved the widow. Without a wise person to go to, the mud could get very thick.

Joseph Hutchinson turned from Israel Porter and walked slowly toward Josiah. Before Josiah could draw back, he rested his big hand on his son's shoulder.

"You have listened carefully here?" he said.

"Aye, sir."

"You've marked it all well?"

"Aye."

"And what say you?"

He's asking what I think! I can't—I can't say it—

But Josiah blocked out that voice and tilted his chin. "I understand, sir," he said clearly.

His father's stern face broke softly into a smile. "Aye," he said quietly. "Aye."

✣ ✢ ✣

Chapter Eighteen

𝔍t was nearly sunset when supper was over. The farm was quiet, all the Hutchinsons busy with their own thoughts. Josiah took his to the pasture where Ninny trotted to him and nuzzled at his neck.

"You've grown tall!" Josiah said.

"Ble-e-h."

"What's that she said?"

Josiah turned to see his father leaning on the fence.

"I—I don't know," Josiah said.

"I think you do. What says the calf?"

Josiah looked into Ninny's brown eyes. "She says she cannot wait to be a cow. There's much confusion in being a calf." Josiah took a breath. "It's like wallowin' in the mud."

Joseph Hutchinson chuckled softly. "Come here, Josiah."

Josiah went to the fence and stood before his father.

"You think," Papa said.

"Sir?"

"Anyone can see that Josiah Hutchinson thinks." He cleared his throat. "It's time you continued your schooling, and since the village can't seem to agree on the where and the when and the how of a school here, Phillip English has suggested that you spend some time with them in Salem Town this summer next and take your schooling there. What say you?"

Josiah felt a light dawning inside him. In all the dark days behind them, he had all but forgotten his dream of the sea. To spend a summer among the ships, tasting the salt air—

"Phillip English sees something in you," his father went on. "Perhaps I see it, too. You've got your mother in you. She only speaks when the need arises." His face creased into a smile. "Perhaps it's best that a man doesn't say everything he's thinking, eh?"

"Aye."

His father tipped his hat. "Think on it, then. And don't stay out past dark."

There was only one place to think on it, and Josiah didn't stop running until he reached the Ipswich River. Panting, he lay down on the grassy bank and closed his eyes. As the last of the sun played on his face, he took out the memories of the day and began to look them over.

Oneko. He was a memory now, but he had been Josiah's best friend. Oneko had known him not by what he said but by what he saw. Josiah smiled to himself. Oneko had known where their house was—had known just where Hope had been the day she left the onion field for her last trip to the widow's. He had known them and loved them for a long time. He wouldn't stop now, even though they would never see him again.

The widow was a memory now, too. But he could almost hear her talking to him, as if they sat with mugs of tea between them. "You have no time to cry over me, Big Squirrel," she would say. "You must be your sister's ears now. Stay quiet and you will hear all you need to for both of you." Hope was right. She would want them to have the cabin—a place to go when the mud got thick and deep.

And then there was the memory of Oneko's father. Josiah shivered. At first he thought perhaps he and Oneko were more alike than he realized. They had almost the same father. But Josiah's father hadn't spat words at Oneko and driven him away as Oneko's father had Hope and Josiah. He didn't hate as the tall Indian did. Joseph Hutchinson understood.

Josiah remembered thinking the day Oneko lay with his eyes closed in the sun that he was praying. His own eyes sprang open now with an idea.

Looking at the memories—that *was* prayer. God was close when Josiah looked back at his day. He didn't give Josiah the words to pray—but He gave him the thoughts to think.

Josiah rolled over on his stomach and looked at his reflection in the water. This was the face of the boy who was going to Salem Town for the summer. For a minute the faces of the Reverend Nicholas Noyes and the red-haired boy and his friends paraded through his mind, but Josiah smiled at the boy in the river. This boy, this Josiah Hutchinson, could handle them now.

Because this boy, this Josiah Hutchinson, was no longer a brainless boy.

✝•✝•✝

1. Lt. John Putnam
2. Widow's Cabin
3. Joseph Putnam
4. Sgt. Putnam
5. Capt. Walcott
6. Rev. Parris
7. Meeting House
8. Hutchinsons' House
9. Nathaniel Putnam
10. Israel Porter
11. Dr. Griggs
12. John Porter's Mill
13. John & Elizabeth Proctor

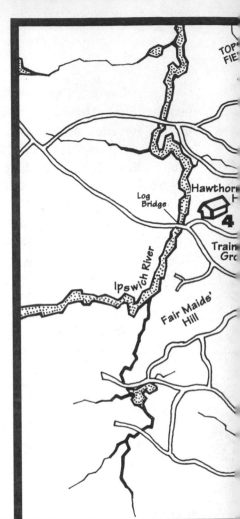

A Map of
SALEM VILLAGE
& Vicinity in 1692

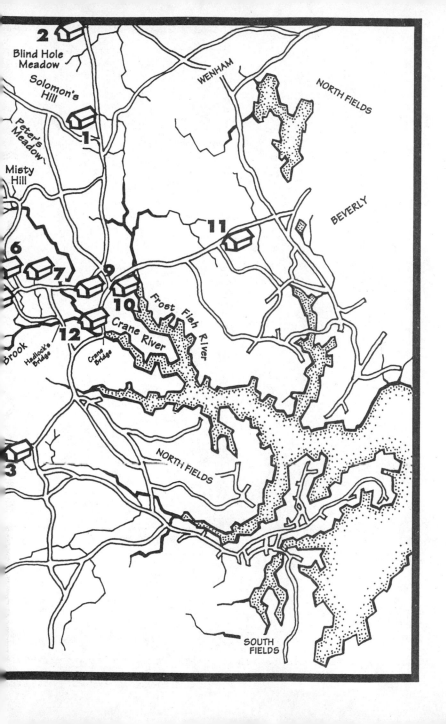